USA TO

TAW

He knows
if you've been
naughty

Studmuffin SANTA

A Ponderosa Resort Romantic Comedy

STUDMUFFIN SANTA

A PONDEROSA RESORT ROMANTIC COMEDY

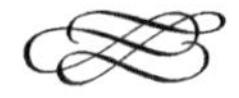

TAWNA FENSKE

This is a work of fiction. Names, characters, organizations, places, events, and incidents are either products of the author's imagination or are used fictitiously.

www.tawnafenske.com

Cover design by Amy Pinkston at wellcoveredbooks.com

ABOUT STUDMUFFIN SANTA

Ugh, Christmas. Not a fan. So why am I wearing a Santa suit and letting frisky moms paw me at a reindeer ranch?

It might have something to do with the family crisis that drew me home between tours as a career Marine. Or maybe it's my urge to cozy up with the prickly reindeer rancher whose curves give me visions of something way hotter than sugarplums.

Jade King isn't thrilled I'm here, and she'd be less thrilled to know her sister hired me to keep an eye on things. Someone's set on sabotaging the ranch, so I've got a built-in excuse to get close to Jade.

I could swear the attraction's mutual, but something's holding her back. Some secret in her past that has her pushing me away like a bad batch of eggnog. It's almost as baffling as all these *accidents* at the King sisters' place. Seriously, who'd screw with a reindeer ranch?

Between sexy Santa suit malfunctions and risqué Christmas cookies, Jade and I keep ending up under the mistletoe together. Is there any chance we can mesh our Christmas wish lists, or will it all crash down like a fat man in a cast iron sleigh?

ALSO IN THE PONDEROSA RESORT ROMANTIC COMEDY SERIES

- Studmuffin Santa
- Chef Sugarlips
- Sergeant Sexypants
- Hottie Lumberjack
- Stiff Suit
- Mancandy Crush (novella)
- Captain Dreamboat
- Snowbound Squeeze (novella)
- Dr. Hot Stuff

If you dig the Ponderosa Resort books, you might also like my Juniper Ridge Romantic Comedy Series. There's even some crossover with characters featured in both worlds. Check it out here:

- Show Time
- Let It Show
- Show Down (coming soon!)
- Just for Show (coming soon!)

- Show and Tell (coming soon!)
- Show of Hands (coming soon!)

For my family, not just the blood relatives, but the ones acquired through marriage or plain dumb luck. Dixie, David, Aaron/Russ, Carlie, Fred, Tamara, Cedar, Violet, and Craig—thanks for the Christmases filled with love, laughter, cheesy holiday movies, recycled gift wrap, inappropriate jokes, and entirely too much sugar. I'm glad you guys are mine.

CHAPTER 1

JADE

"Here's a little secret, woman to woman." I lean closer, making sure I have her undivided attention. "It's the small things that make a difference. A good mani/pedi, maybe sprucing up your hair a bit? The boys are going to notice."

The lady in question shoots me a dubious look but says nothing.

That's probably because I'm the last person who should give dating advice.

Also, because she's a reindeer.

"Come on," I coax, lifting Tammy's back hoof. "Just let me trim the edge, and you'll be all set. I promise I won't nip the quick this time."

Tammy responds by trying to lie down in the chute, which is the opposite of helpful. "You were a lot more cooperative when you were in heat."

A familiar laugh rings through the barn, and I turn to see my sister skipping into the pen wearing a red and green Christmas sweater. I swear Amber owns at least sixty of them, and they're on constant rotation this time of year.

"If by 'cooperative' you mean 'trying to hump everything in

sight,' you're spot-on," she says. "Didn't she put the moves on the feed trough last time she was in heat?"

"You can't judge a girl when she's desperate."

"True enough," Amber says, reaching out to scratch Tammy behind her right ear. "I thought you didn't trim hooves unless their antlers are in the soft stage."

"I don't, but she had a cracked hoof, and I can't get the farrier out until next Saturday. Come on, help me hold her."

Amber moves to the front of the chute to coo in Tammy's ear. "Don't worry, girl," she murmurs. "We're going with artificial insemination next time. No more awkward humping from Harold."

"We should probably start calling them by their stage names now that it's November," I point out as I snip the edge of Tammy's—make that Dasher's—hoof. "And dial back the sex talk. Our first kiddie field trip shows up in an hour. They don't need to hear about humping."

"Actually, I think humping is the first thing they'd want to hear about," Amber points out as I turn Tammy's hoof to get the other side. "That and pooping. You'll make the kids' week if you can work more bodily functions into your reindeer presentations."

I sigh and snip again. "Maybe not the image we want to put out there for Jingle Bell Reindeer Ranch. Please tell me you've channeled that marketing degree into something more helpful."

My sister beams and holds Tammy's head a little tighter as the reindeer struggles to halt the pedicure. "That's what I came to tell you, actually. Some fabulous news."

"Oh yeah? You talked them out of hosting weddings at *Ponderosa Luxury Ranch Resort?*"

I deliver those last four words with my best socialite sneer, which would be a more convincing impersonation if I weren't dressed in muddy flannel and knee-high rubber boots. My sister shakes her head.

"Not yet. I have a meeting next week with their marketing person. Maybe I'll convince them to ditch that plan."

"Try undoing a couple buttons on your top."

"She's a woman, so no."

"Don't rule it out." I set Tammy's left hoof down gently, then reach for the right. She gives a little kick, but my grip is firm, and she eventually settles in. I start snipping again, working my way carefully around the edges. "So what did you come to tell me?"

"The best news," Amber says. "Awesome news!" She pauses for dramatic effect, and I glance up to see her cheeks are rosy with excitement. "I hired Santa."

She bounces on her heels, her holiday cheer more contagious than mumps. I catch myself starting to smile. "From the way you're acting, you either hired Brad Pitt or you made out with him in the tack room," I observe. "Maybe both."

"Please." She rolls her eyes at me as I set down Tammy's hoof and give her a gentle pat on the rump. Amber lets go of the reindeer's neck and plants a kiss on her cheek, expertly dodging Tammy's massive, branchlike antlers.

Amber pulls the lever to release the chute. "You're free!" she sings as Tammy gallops into the pasture, bounding like a kitten mainlining catnip. "That's pretty much how I felt breaking up with Zak last week," my sister mutters as she turns back to me.

"You mean *this* time?" My sister and her boyfriend split up more often than most people change socks, but I have to admit it seems to be sticking.

"I'm serious this time," she says. "I'm focusing three-hundred percent on the reindeer ranch. No more men for me right now, even if he did look like Clooney."

I can relate, though not for the same reasons. Let's just say I didn't have the best early experiences with the opposite sex. Besides, getting Jingle Bell Ranch up and running is my number one priority, so I sure as hell don't have time for dating.

Amber's distracted watching Sydney and Edward—stage

names Prancer and Cupid—try to rub velvet off each other's antlers, so I nudge her with my elbow. "So what's the deal with Santa?" I ask. "Did you land that old guy from the bank with the big white beard and the weird halitosis?"

"Ew, and no." She makes a face. "Even with a box of Tic Tacs, that guy was like a fire-breathing dragon."

"Dragon Santa." I shake my head and shove the snippers into the pocket of my Carharts. "Not the marketing hook we want."

"Plus, he wanted twice what we're willing to pay," she says. "Told me the authentic beard was worth more than a fake one, and he should get the same sort of bonus strippers get for real boobs instead of fake ones."

"That's a thing?"

Amber shrugs. "How should I know? We didn't cover stripper economics in my business classes."

"That's a shame. Might be a good fallback career." Randy, one of this season's reindeer calves, comes wandering up to sniff my pockets for apples, and I give him a scratch behind one stubby antler. "So who's Santa? Don't tell me you picked that other guy —the one with the résumé covered in little foil bells who said he's trying to change his legal name to Saint Nick."

"Ugh. His background check came back with three counts of indecent exposure and anyway, ew—*no*. Come on, Jade. Are you going to let me tell you, or are we going to play guessing games all day?"

"I was kind of enjoying the games," I admit. "Fine. Who's Santa?"

Amber smiles like a cat stealing licks from the butter dish and tosses her long, dark hair. "Brandon Brown."

I laugh and rummage through my pocket for a baby-sized apple as Randy noses me again. "That's funny, I went to school with a Brandon Brown. Remember how the football announcer yelled his name through the PA like he was proclaiming a God's descent from Mt. Olympus? 'Now taking the field, quarterback Brandon Brown. All hail!'"

The mental picture of Wonder Boy Brandon Brown strutting across a football field with a ball under one arm and a Santa hat on his head makes me laugh out loud.

It takes me a second to realize Amber isn't laughing.

"Um, yes, actually," she says, scuffing her boot through the dirt. "Same guy."

I stop laughing. "You can't be serious. He's *our* age, not Santa material."

Amber rolls her eyes at me. "He was a senior when you were a freshman and I was in grade school, but why the hell does that matter? Kids aren't going to check his ID."

"Santa's *old*," I point out, pretty sure I'm arguing the wrong point. There's a damn good reason I don't love the idea of inviting a former king of the jocks to my ranch, and it has nothing to do with Santa's age.

"That's what they make fake beards for," Amber says. "And strap-on bellies. I already ordered one for him."

I close my eyes and count to ten, but only make it to four. "Please tell me you read the product description instead of googling 'Santa strap-on.'"

"Will you relax? Jeez, I learned my lesson with the leather harness that turned out not to be for reindeer."

"Yeah, Blitzen's still pissed about the ball gag," I mutter. "Did you seriously hire the king of the asshole jocks to be Santa?"

"It's been thirteen years since he graduated," she points out. "I'm guessing he's gotten over himself being in the Marines for more than a decade."

I consider pointing out that I'm not entirely over the mean-spirited teasing hurled at me by the jocks and princesses in Brandon's circle of friends. Five years younger than me, and blessedly spared the baby fat that clung to me through my teens, Amber was unaware of the torment I endured in my high school years. I'd just as soon keep it that way.

"Why Brandon Brown?" I ask. "Why not get someone who looks the part?"

"Oh, he looks the part, all right." Amber grins. "He looks like a freakin' Chippendale dancer."

I stare at my sister, not sure whether to box her ears or whack her in the arm with a sock full of hot nickels. "How is this helpful? You think a bunch of people want to show up and gawk at Old Saint Nick, who, by the way, is some stupid-hot Marine who couldn't look less Santa-like if he tried?"

The second the words leave my mouth, I realize that's exactly what my sister thinks. And that she's convinced it's a *good* thing.

"Come on," Amber says. "Who usually brings the kiddies to pet the reindeer and see Santa? The moms, right?"

"Right," I say slowly.

"Rumors spread fast around here," she points out. "Once word gets out that Santa looks like Chris Hemsworth, we'll have every mommy in a sixty-mile radius lining up to sit on his lap."

"You mean put their *kids* on his lap," I grumble. "This is a family attraction, remember?"

"I know, I know." She waves a dismissive hand like that's a minor detail, which maybe it is according to her plan. "But you asked me to help put Jingle Bell Reindeer Ranch on the map. To make us super-profitable in the winter months so we can keep these guys in apples and hay for the rest of the year, right?"

I nod, though I'm not sure how that request translates to having Brandon Brown here on my ranch. We're making good progress toward our goal of running a successful business, and I sure as hell don't need some Wonder Boy ex-jock turning us into a beefcake circus.

"I thought he was on active duty somewhere," I say.

"He's taking some sort of extended military family leave

thing," she says. "I don't know the details, but he'll be home for a couple months."

I sigh, not sure which of my objections to raise next. "Look, I appreciate what you're trying to do," I say. "But I don't think Studmuffin Santa is the way to go."

"Studmuffin Santa, huh?" The rumble of a male voice over my shoulder makes me spin around so fast I nearly twist an ankle.

But Brandon Brown is there to catch me, his musclebound arms looking like something he ripped off a life-sized G.I. Joe action figure.

I recognize him in an instant, even though I haven't laid eyes on him for thirteen years. He has the same tousled mop of sandy hair and eyes like melty puddles of pine-green crayon that had all the high school cheerleaders lining up to toss their panties at him.

I was never a cheerleader. I was president of the Future Farmers of America.

Only, right now, I'm not feeling very presidential. I'm feeling unhinged. I'm feeling flushed. I'm feeling Brandon Brown's hands on my arms and liking it a lot more than I should.

"You must be the boss," he says with a voice that prompts swooning from every female in a ten-foot radius, reindeer included. "I'm Brandon, but I guess you should call me Santa. Or was it Studmuffin Santa?"

His eyes are teasing, and his hands are massive around my biceps. I swallow hard and try to find my voice.

"Studmuffin Santa," I repeat. "Welcome to Jingle Bell Reindeer Ranch."

CHAPTER 2

BRANDON

It occurs to me that I should probably take my hands off my new boss.

The dawning of this thought and my brain's ability to execute the action are separated by about ten seconds, which makes for an awkward first meeting.

"Brandon Brown," she says. She licks her lips and stares at me like I stood her up for prom, which I'm positive never happened.

Almost positive.

No, I'm *totally* positive. I'd remember those lake blue eyes for sure. Not just any lake, either. Crater Lake, where I worked the summer between high school and the Marines. It's the deepest lake in the U.S., and tourists would ask what kind of dye we used to make the water so blue. *"Just pure water, ma'am,"* I'd say with a touch of small-town Oregon twang that charmed the pants off many a young college girl that summer. *"Purest water there is."*

This girl's eyes are like that.

Like that, but pissed off. She's staring at me like I just tracked dog doo on her carpet, so I decide to keep my mouth shut about lakes or college girls or anything else that might get me into trouble.

"I'm Jade King," she says. "I think maybe there's been a misunderst—"

"My sister is delighted you've agreed to be our Santa this season." The brunette I met earlier—Amber?—edges between us like an overzealous referee and elbows Jade in the ribs. "I was just telling her how much you love Christmas and how excited you are to be part of the team spreading holiday cheer at Jingle Bell Ranch."

Every word of that is bullshit, from my supposed love of the most commercialized holiday on earth to Jade's fictional excitement about me being here.

But since Amber has set the Liar-mobile in motion, I press the gas pedal. "It's nice to finally meet you, Jade. I've heard great things about you."

I can tell from her expression that's the wrong thing to say, though I have no idea why.

"Oh?" She cocks her head to the side and gives me a skeptical look. "Like what have you heard?"

Shit.

"Um, well, that you're capable and strong and really skilled on a farm."

Great, I've just made her sound like a draft horse.

Sweating, I try again. "Look, Amber told me to come by at two to meet you in person and fill out some paperwork," I say. "But I can come back another time if now's not good for you."

I shut my mouth so I don't repeat the rest of what Amber told me. That she's worried about odd stuff happening here—tools gone missing, gates left open, an eerie feeling of being watched—and that older sister Jade would never consent to professional security. Kinda kills the festive family vibe.

A Santa who fills the role in a subtle way seemed like a solution, so here I am.

Jade stares at me for a moment with those Crater Lake eyes unblinking. Two shaggy reindeer stand behind her with antlers the size of coat racks, looking like thugs poised to beat the shit out of me if Jade gives the order.

But she seems to decide something then, and spins on her heel to walk away. I do not check out her ass because I am a gentleman. Also because the tail of her plaid flannel shirt comes down past her hips.

But mostly because I'm a gentleman.

"Come on," she calls over her shoulder. "You can walk with me while I check the fence line."

I'm not sure what we're checking it for or why I'm already taking orders from her when I'm not positive I have this job. But I've got nothing better to do on this cold November afternoon, so I fall in beside her and try not to step on any piles of little black berries I'm ninety percent sure aren't berries.

Jade's walking fast for a girl almost a foot shorter than me, but she's not breathing hard at all. She's also not looking at me.

"So we're the third largest domesticated reindeer herd in the continental U.S." She stops and adjusts something on a surprisingly tall fence, then continues on like the world's least-friendly tour guide. "A lot of them came from abusive homes or neglect situations, so I've been doing rehab with them and getting them ready to interact with the public."

I want to ask what reindeer rehab entails, but I suspect she'd think I'm making fun of her. "They look good to me," I offer. "Not that I know what healthy reindeer look like, but I assume they are. Healthy, that is."

I'm spewing word salad like it's on the menu, which isn't like me at all. I'm usually pretty polished around women, so I don't know why this one's making me blather like a moron.

Jade spares me a glance and continues walking. "They *are* healthy. We had four new calves born last spring, which gives us fourteen steers, sixteen cows, and one bull who's not going to be a bull much longer."

I'm almost afraid to ask. "What do you mean?"

She gives me a pointed look. "Harold—stage name Donner—is getting castrated next week."

"Ouch."

Jade shrugs and keeps walking. "Bulls are impossible to deal with during rut. Nonstop grunting from August to December, and they're mean as hell. Dangerous, too."

"I've known guys like that."

Jade stops walking again and turns to face me. She narrows her eyes just a little, and I fight the urge to take a step back. "They die young," she says. "Reindeer bulls do. You get three or four breeding seasons out of them, and they might live a year or so after that, but not much. Unless you castrate them, they're pretty much goners."

"Jesus."

I'm not sure we're still talking about reindeer, but I don't love the way she just glanced at my crotch. Or maybe I'm imagining things. "So you're cutting off his balls to save his life."

"Pretty much." Jade starts walking again. "Artificial insemination's better for the herd anyway. Safer, too. Each reindeer is worth about ten grand, so we can't afford to lose one to a hookup gone bad."

That explains her hostility about mating. Maybe. It also explains why Amber was so gung-ho to have security. Now that I've met Jade, I understand why Amber said her sister would bristle at accepting outside help. I get the sense Jade would happily punch me in the jaw if I offered to carry her groceries.

I glance around the pasture, wondering which one's the bull and whether I should go offer my condolences. "Have you always had reindeer?"

"No." She pauses as a particularly massive specimen lumbers up and noses her pocket. I'm standing close enough that his antlers bump my arm, and I'm surprised by how powerful they are. Jade reaches into her pocket and pulls out the tiniest apple I've ever seen, which she gives him along with an ear scratch.

"The land has been in my family for six generations, but it's been a few different things," she says. "My parents raised pigs when I was growing up." She glances at me like she's daring me to say something about that, but I have no interest in taking that dare. "They sold off the pigs when they retired to Hawaii," she continues. "Now the farm belongs to my sister and me."

"So you decided to start a reindeer ranch," I say. "Something different."

She keeps walking, but I see her nod once. "A little different. It's a commercial operation, obviously, but we're still maintaining the regional culture and the intended purpose of the land."

"Okay," I say, though I have no idea what she's talking about. "I guess you've gotta do what it takes to make farmland profitable these days."

She stops walking and frowns up at me. "That's not entirely true. These properties were meant to be farms and ranches. You couldn't just plunk down a shopping mall or a strip club or some fancy resort for rich people. Not without losing the integrity of the land."

Oh.

Okay, now I know what she's talking about.

"You mean that luxury ranch resort thing down the road? The one opening next fall?"

She doesn't answer right away. Just keeps walking, pausing once to check a sturdy-looking gate before continuing her march along the fence line. Her hair is long and wavy like her sister's, but streaked with honey-colored rays of sunshine. A breeze catches the end of her ponytail, sending the soft strands fluttering across my forearm.

"I'm saying it's important to be respectful of established culture and tradition," she says. "Out here in the country, there are issues like grazing rights and quality of life and traffic patterns and—"

"Hey, I grew up here, too. I get it, don't worry."

That gets a snort out of her. "Yeah, well I'm not sure the resort people do. Out-of-state billionaires snapping up family farms and turning them into Disneyland for rich people? No, thanks."

"I can introduce you to them, if you want," I offer as she stoops to study a snag on some wire. "The Bracelyn family? They're my cousins."

She stands up so fast she smacks the top of her head on my elbow, which makes her teeter in tall rubber boots. I reach out without thinking and catch her arms again, annoyed to realize how much I like it.

For the second time in fifteen minutes, I force myself to unhand the boss.

Her throat moves as she swallows, and those lake blue eyes stare up at me in dismay. "You're related to the Bracelyns?"

"Yeah," I say slowly. "On my dad's side. My uncle was the out-of-state billionaire. He bought it when I was a kid, but didn't visit much until after my mom—"

Fuck.

I stop talking, not sure what's got me blathering my life story to someone I've just met. Jade's eyes are like magnets, drawing sharp shards of steel out of the scarred ridges on my chest.

I force myself to swallow. "Anyway, I'm staying out there with my cousins right now," I continue. "I can talk to them if you want."

She looks like she wants to dig a hole under the fence and make a run for it, but instead she turns and abruptly starts walking again. "I didn't know that," she mumbles. "That you're related to the Bracelyns."

"How would you? We have different last names, and it's not like I put it on my job application."

"Of course not, but we went to high school together."

"You and me? We did?"

She doesn't look at me, but I could swear she just rolled her eyes. She's walking faster now, so I hurry to keep up as I rack my brain trying to remember her.

Our high school wasn't huge—maybe fifteen-hundred students—but I'd definitely remember a girl with lake blue eyes and an attitude like a blast of rocket fire.

"We didn't know each other in school," she says at last. "I knew *of* you, but didn't everyone?"

"Because of the sports stuff," I ask, "or because I was an asshole?"

She fires me a curious look. "Did you just call yourself an asshole?"

I shrug. "I can admit it now. I was kind of a dick in high school. Might as well take the bull by the horns. Or the reindeer."

That gets a smile out of her. A small one I see only in profile, but still a smile.

"Antlers," she says at last. "Reindeer have antlers, not horns."

"I'll remember that."

"Do." She stops and turns to face me, her chin tilted up. "And keep in mind they're more dangerous than they look. A reindeer can kill a full-grown man with just a flick of its head, if the mood strikes."

I take a deep breath and nod. "I'll consider myself warned."

CHAPTER 3

JADE

"So that's how reindeer grow a new set of antlers every single year," I conclude, proud of myself for making it through our eighth and final field trip of the week. "Are there any questions?"

A little boy in a blue coat raises his hand at the front of the pack. "What are those two reindeers doing?"

There's a titter of giggles from the pack of seven-year-olds standing along my fence line, and I turn to survey where he's pointing. Beside the barn, a confused-looking steer is doing his best to mount one of the young females. She turns and butts him with her antlers, but Lester is undeterred.

"He's—uh—yes," I stammer. "Leapfrog. They're playing leapfrog."

"He's not very good at it," observes a little blonde girl in pigtails and purple sneakers.

"In his defense, he's missing the parts he'd need to be an effective player," I point out.

Their teacher gives me a nervous look, and I make a mental note to dab Vicks VapoRub on all females who go into heat between now and Christmas. It's an old trick for keeping the boys away, though judging by the determination on Lester's face, it might not be enough.

"Okay, I think we're just about out of time," I announce. "Thank you for coming to Jingle Bell Reindeer Ranch. Don't forget to ask your parents to bring you back next week when we have Santa here."

Santa!

The word ripples through the crowd of school-kids with a hushed excitement, and everyone starts talking at once about Christmas lists and presents and how often the big man in red needs to stop the sleigh and poop after eating all those cookies.

The students' teacher, Stacey Fleming, sidles up to me. She's a pretty blonde who was two years ahead of me in school, but through the magic of makeup and good genes, she looks about ten years younger. Her hair is that shoulder-length, flippy style meant to look effortless, but requiring two hours of intense labor with a curling iron. At least it would for me, which is why I stick with a ponytail most days.

Stacey's wearing red leather knee-high boots that she's somehow managed to keep mud-free, and her white peasant blouse is spotless. I wonder if she remembers the time in junior high when one of her friends stole a Twinkie out of my lunchbox and ran away giggling about how I didn't need the extra calories.

"Thanks again for doing this," Stacey says as the kids file toward the front of the school bus where my sister has set up a snack table. "The students had a great time."

"No problem," I say. "It's nice to get to show them how the farm works. What the reindeer eat and how they look instead of the cartoon pictures of them on TV."

Stacey smiles and leans in with a conspiratorial whisper. "So what are they really?"

"What are what?" I whisper back, totally clueless.

"What are the animals? Some sort of elk or something?"

I resist the urge to roll my eyes. It's not the first time I've encountered someone who lumps unicorns and reindeer together in the class of mythical beasts, but I might have hoped a teacher would know better.

"They're reindeer," I tell her. "Real, honest-to-goodness reindeer."

She nods and gives me a knowing smile. "Ah, got it." She winks. "Your secret's safe with me."

I start to protest, but think better of it and shut my mouth. If she wants to believe I'm passing off fake reindeer to the public, there's not much I can do about it.

Stacey's eyes go wide, and it takes me a second to notice she's not looking at me or the reindeer. She's staring at the parking lot over my shoulder. "Oh my God," she whispers. "Is that Brandon Brown?"

The name sends goosebumps skittering up my arms, but I turn slowly, trying not to show the same awestruck eagerness as Stacey. I fix my expression in a nonchalant gaze I feel wavering when I see him striding up my driveway in a fitted black T-shirt and jeans that make me want to pen a thank you note to Levi Strauss.

"Yep," I say, still striving for casual but unable to hide the wobble in my voice. "He's probably here to pick up his uniform. His first day as Santa is next week."

"*That's* your Santa?"

Her voice is practically a shriek, and I glance toward the bus to make sure none of the kids heard. They're all distracted by the paper mugs of cocoa Amber is handing out, along with generous squirts of hand sanitizer. I turn back to Stacey.

"Apparently so," I tell her. "I just got his background check, and everything looked fine."

"I'll say things look fine." She's watching Brandon, not me, and I can't tell if her expression is one of pleasure or irritation. Maybe a bit of both.

"You know him?" I ask.

"Biblically," she murmurs, voice still teetering between annoyance and attraction.

He has that effect on me, too.

A tiny inchworm of jealousy wiggles around in my gut, but I ignore it the same way I'm trying to ignore the gentleness in Brandon's eyes as he stops to pet Anthony, one of the smallest steers in my herd.

A flicker of memory lights up my brain, an image of Brandon jogging off the field and dropping his helmet on the sidelines as Stacey leapt into his arms, wrapping herself around him in her cheerleading skirt. "You guys dated in high school," I say.

Stacey shrugs. "I wouldn't say dated. He took me out a couple times." She gives a brittle little laugh. "Me and everyone else with a perky pair of tits."

I ignore what may or may not have been a jab at my teenage rack. It wasn't until senior year that my baby fat rearranged itself into something resembling curves. Brandon had long since graduated by then, and it's not like we'd have run in the same circles regardless of my boobage.

Brandon stops petting the reindeer and strides toward us, probably all too familiar with what it looks like when two women are trying to pretend they aren't discussing him.

"Hey, Jade, Stacey. Good to see you again."

His stride is slow and cocky like he knows he's God's gift to denim. His t-shirt is short-sleeved, despite the fact the it's freakin' November in Central Oregon. I don't know whether I hate him more for not being cold or for having biceps that make my mouth water.

"Hey, Brandon," Stacey purrs. "I didn't know you were back in town. Last I heard you were in Syria someplace."

"Just finished my last tour in Raqqa," he says. "I had a ton of accumulated leave to burn, so I'm here through the holidays."

"So it's just temporary?"

He shrugs and looks away. "I'm considering leaving the

service." He drags his boot through the dirt. "I'm a little war weary, plus I've got some family stuff going on."

She smiles and sidles up closer, surveying him the way my reindeer eye a bucket of apples. "I'd love to hear about what you've been up to. Maybe we could grab a drink sometime?"

Brandon clears his throat. "Actually, I'm going to be pretty busy with Jade here."

There's an uncomfortable silence as Stacey looks from Brandon to me and back to Brandon, probably humming the *Sesame Street* song, "One of These Things is not Like the Other" in the back of her mind.

"Playing Santa," I clarify, wanting to make it clear we're not an item. Not that anyone in their right mind would think that.

Stacey nods once, then turns back to Brandon. "You're looking good, Bran," she says. "I'll see you around."

Leave it to Stacey to turn fiber cereal into a nickname and make it sound sexy. She turns and saunters away, her butt blinking with those sparkly crystals that adorn the pockets of some women's jeans. Not mine, obviously. My butt has never twinkled, and I wonder if that should be a point of pride or regret.

Stacey rejoins her class, rumpling hair and talking to kids whose faces are smudged with cocoa and mud. At least I hope it's mud. She chats with the kids for a while before stepping over to talk to Amber. My sister points toward the hay barn, probably telling her where the restroom is, and I watch as Stacey ambles in that direction.

I turn back to Brandon, assuming he's been looking at her like I have. But nope, his gaze is fixed on me.

"I like your hair like that," he says.

"Unwashed and unbrushed?" I flip my low ponytail over one shoulder. "Thanks."

He grins. "Anyone ever tell you that you suck at taking a compliment?"

"Anyone ever tell you it's a bad idea to tell your new boss she sucks?"

Brandon shakes his head. "According to that PI guy you had doing my background check, you're not technically my boss. He was real adamant about telling me it's your sister."

"Ugh." I give him an Amber-esque eyeroll. "That's Connor, and he's been madly in love with Amber for years. I'm sure he's just trying to pee on her fire hydrant."

"You can promise him I'm not the least bit interested in lifting my leg on your sister."

"That's reassuring. Her ex-boyfriend, Zak, is our photographer this year, so you'd have to get through him, too." I pluck a stray piece of alfalfa off the end of my ponytail and wonder how long it's been there. "I guess you're here to try on the Santa suit?"

Anthony the reindeer steer nudges Brandon's hand with his nose, and Brandon strokes his neck again. Not the most subtle request for affection, but effective.

"I'm sure the Santa suit is fine," Brandon says. "Aren't these things kinda one size fits all?"

"You seem a little bigger than average."

The second the words leave my mouth, I want to snatch them back and shove them under the water trough. I expect a smug response from Wonder Boy, but he doesn't smirk at all. Not even a smile. Just clears his throat and taps the toe of his boot on my fencepost.

"I pulled out my yearbooks last night," he says. "You were cute. How come we didn't know each other in high school?"

"Because all cute girls should be required to throw themselves at you?"

He laughs. "Are you always this touchy?"

"Are you always this cocky?"

"Yeah," he says, his tone oddly sheepish. "But I'm working on that."

I'm not sure what to say to that, since I can't tell if he's kidding. I realize I didn't acknowledge his "cute" remark, but it feels weird now to thank him for a compliment I'm not sure he meant.

Besides, there's nothing cute about that yearbook photo. My cheeks were plump and my eyes too bright, prompting someone to scribble "Miss Piggy" when I left my yearbook unattended in the lunch room.

He probably has no idea about any of that, I remind myself.

"We ran in different circles in high school," I say, wondering if I really need to point out that there's little overlap between the awkward farm girl circle and the untouchable sports god circle. "And you disappeared pretty fast after graduation."

"You noticed?" His brows lift in genuine curiosity, and I wonder why it would be any surprise to him that the whole town has been hanging on his every achievement.

I shrug and try to pretend I didn't just admit to watching for him anytime I knew he'd be home on leave. I never spoke his name or asked around about how he was doing, but I did keep an eye out at the grocery store, snatching bits of gossip like a squirrel gathering acorns.

"Sure," I say. "The paper ran articles every now and then about where you were getting deployed and how many medals you won. Hometown Hero and all that."

He smiles. "It's good to be home."

Something about the word *home* gives me a funny feeling in the pit of my belly, and I turn away from him before he can read the nostalgia on my face. "Come on," I tell him. "Let's get you undressed. Dressed. Whatever."

I stalk away from him before he can notice my flaming cheeks. What is it about this guy that turns me into a tongue-tied sexual harasser?

I lead him into the south barn, the one we've been renovating to host holiday events and our meet and greets with Santa. Pushing open the door, I breathe in the scent of sweet hay and rehydrated beet pellets and my whole childhood. Brandon steps through the threshold, and I pull the door closed behind us before continuing toward the opposite end of the barn.

"There's your throne." I point to the massive oak chair festooned with red garland and bits of holly. It gleams like a showpiece under the window, the tufted velvet cushion waiting to cup Santa's perfect ass.

Stop thinking about Santa's ass.

Brandon takes a step toward the chair, bringing his ass back into view and thwarting my plan to stop ogling him.

"This is the Santa chair?" He runs his hand over the arm, making me shiver with the memory of his hands on my arms. "Where'd you get this?"

"Amber found it at an antique store in Terrebonne. We had to strip off all the old paint to get to bare wood. It took us a month to get it sanded down and refinished."

"It's beautiful."

"Thanks." There's a niggle of pride in my throat, and I swallow hard to get it down. "The hardware is all original."

Brandon strokes one of the sleek honey-gold spindles. "It's amazing. Way cooler than that ratty-looking easy chair they had at Cascade Mall."

"You remember that?" I laugh, surprised that I do, too. "It always smelled like rotting meat."

"I thought that was Santa," he said. "For years, I associated St. Nick with decomposing bodies."

"Now there's a childhood memory guaranteed to mess up all your future Christmases."

Is it my imagination, or did something just shift in his expression? It's faint, and I probably wouldn't notice at all if I weren't staring at his face like I'm worried it'll melt away. It's like a cloud passing by the sun, and his gaze snags on mine and holds for a few seconds. I feel like a yellowjacket trapped in a jar of congealed cola.

"Come on," he says. "Let's find that suit."

He turns and heads toward the back corner before seeming to recall he doesn't know where he's going. He stops and looks back at me with something oddly vulnerable in his expression.

"No, you're right," I say, hustling to catch up. "It's this way."

I head toward the office, moving around the small pen we've built to hold the reindeer that are part of Santa's display. There's an empty Christmas tree stand beside that, and I remind myself to go spruce hunting sometime in the next week.

"Right through here," I say as I tug open the door to the cramped space that serves as my office. The box containing the Santa suit is right on the edge, so I lift out the bundle of red velvet and faux fur and hand it to him.

"We weren't sure about size, so we got a couple different things so you can mix and match."

"Thank you." The bell on the tip of the hat gives a soft jingle, and my heart does an awkward shimmy as Brandon's fingers graze mine. "Where should I change?"

"In here's fine," I say. "There's a lock on the door and everything."

That earns me a curious eyebrow quirk, and I wonder if he's pondering the likelihood of me barging in while he's naked.

I keep my expression flat, like illicit thoughts aren't scurrying through my brain like rabbits in heat.

Brandon nods and sets the bundle back down on the desk. Before I can move out of the way, he's grabbed the hem of his T-shirt and started to lift it over his head.

"I'll—uh—be right out here," I stammer, backing out of the room so fast I trip over my feet. I slam the door behind me, cheeks hot enough to fry bacon on my face.

What the hell is wrong with me?

I move away from the office and busy myself rearranging hay bales, lugging them from one side of the display to the other. It's heavy work, and I end up yanking off my plaid flannel so I'm down to just my favorite Wonder Woman tee.

Once the hay is moved, I fuss with the garland that Amber and I strung around some exposed beams. Then I fluff the Santa cushion, doing my damnedest not to think about Santa's fine posterior.

"Uh, Jade?"

I jerk up at the sound of Brandon's voice. "Yeah?"

"I'm having trouble with the suit."

His voice is muffled on the other side of the office door, and I step closer so I can hear him.

"What sort of trouble?" I call.

"There's this thing I can't figure out—"

"The belt?"

He makes an exasperated noise. "I think I know how a belt works."

The office door opens, and out steps Brandon. He's wearing black boots and red velvet pants and—actually, I'm just guessing what's below the waist.

Because I'm gawking like an idiot at what's above the waist.

The red velvet coat gapes open in the middle, exposing a wide swath of bare chest dusted with fine, golden hair. Below that, the world's most perfect abs form a delicious row of speedbumps leading to the happiest happy trail I've ever laid eyes on. I swallow hard, unable to take my eyes off it. Off *him*.

"Jade."

His voice hurls a spear of desire straight through my chest, and I'm having trouble breathing. I rip my gaze off his abdomen and force myself to look him in the eye.

Big mistake. Those dark, pine-green puddles turn my tongue to chalk, and I can't seem to make my voice work.

"Uh-huh?" I manage.

"I need to borrow your hands for a sec."

Oh, dear God.

CHAPTER 4

BRANDON

I take a step toward Jade and notice she takes a step back. Her eyes are fixed on my pecs, and I glance down to make sure I'm not sporting a hideous chest zit or something.

No zit.

Which means Jade—the ice queen who hasn't given me the time of day since I set foot on this farm—is checking me out.

Before I get too smug about that, I remind myself that the sight of her in a fitted blue T-shirt with a winged W on the chest has just confirmed what I've suspected from day one. Jade King has a killer body. Lush curves and narrow waist and the sort of well-muscled arms I can't stop picturing wrapped around my back.

I swallow hard, trying to get my bearings. I came out here for some reason, but damned if I can remember now what it was.

"Why are you holding that like it's a dead animal?" she asks.

I look down at my hand, relieved to see I am not, in fact, holding a dead animal. I think. I have no idea what the hell it is, so I heft up the weird-looking padded thing with strings on it.

"Is this some sort of chest protection like a catcher would wear? Or a butt pad for Santas who have to sit all day?"

Jade laughs, and it's the sweetest sound I've ever heard. She steps closer, and for a second, I think she's going to touch my chest. I hold my breath, aching for that moment her hand brushes my bare skin.

But no, she reaches for the padded thing instead. "This is your belly," she says.

"My what?"

"Your belly," she repeats. "Like a bowl full of jelly?"

She looks at me like she's explaining something to an exceptionally dense toddler, and I get lost in those blue eyes again. What was she saying?

"Jelly," I repeat.

"Of course. Santa's supposed to be a little squishy in the middle, but uh—obviously you're not, so—"

"Fake belly."

"Right." Her gaze skims quickly over my abs, and I resist the urge to flex. I want her to look. I want her to touch, honestly. I want the excuse to take her in my arms and—

"Take off your jacket," she commands.

"What?"

"Your Santa jacket," she says. "You need to take it off."

I don't ask questions, willing to shed any article of clothing she asks me to. I hang the Santa coat on a nail sticking out of the post beside me as Jade fiddles with the buckles on the belly pad.

"Do I need to take off my pants?" I ask.

"What? No! No pants. Please, keep your pants on!"

I try not to take offense at the horrified look on her face, or the fact that she just took another step away from me. Maybe she needs more room to tinker with the strings on the belly device. Her fingers work the straps with impressive deftness, and I admire the curve of her neck as she bends over her work. What would it be like to kiss her there? To skim a fingertip from the soft place behind her ear all the way down to her collarbone. To brush my lips along her hairline. Would she shiver at my touch, or slap my hand away?

"Here," she says, hoisting up the belly device. "It loops around your neck and then ties in back. Try this."

I duck into the neck loop, conscious of her breasts grazing my ribs through her fitted tee. Her hair tickles my shoulder, and I breathe in the fragrant scent of hay and juniper berries and something sweet. Honey, I think, or gingerbread. Or maybe that's just Jade.

She steps back, and I open my eyes, surprised to discover I've closed them in the first place.

"Hang on, let me help with the ties."

"Thanks," I manage to croak as she wraps her arms around my waist. I lift my arms up, not sure if it's more to get them out of her way or to keep myself from touching her.

Her whole body presses close to mine as she cinches the laces around my torso. "God, it's like a corset or something," she mutters as her fingers flutter against my lower back.

"Not a very convenient design," I manage to reply, a little lightheaded from her closeness. "How's Santa supposed to get dressed by himself? Or undressed, for that matter?"

"Maybe they figure you'll have a whole team of elves helping you," she says. "Hang on, let me try it from the other side."

She moves behind me, and the tip of her ponytail grazes my ribs. I suck in a breath, not sure why I'm ticklish when I never have been before. It must be her, then, Jade with her sweet-smelling hair and graceful hands and mouthwatering curves and—

"That's quite the tattoo," she says.

Her hand grazes my compass, and I hold my breath wanting her to trace every line with her fingers. It's a big tattoo.

"I got it in Baghdad," I say. "It's pointing the direction home."

"Did it hurt?"

"Not as much as the shrapnel it's covering."

"Oh," she says softly. "Sorry. And, um—thank you for your service."

I nod, not sure why I'm feeling so undone. It's not like I've never had a beautiful woman look at me before. It's not like I've never had female hands raking my torso, so why the hell do Jade's make me so jumpy?

Because she's different.

I swallow hard, praying she'll get a knot in the laces. That she'll have some reason to stay back there forever, butterfly fingertips brushing my back as her breath fans my shoulder blades.

"There," she announces as she moves away. "How does that feel?"

I turn to face her, socked full-force in the gut by those lake-blue eyes. God. I need to stop this. I look down at the fake belly, hoping my desire will be dampened by the fact that I look utterly ridiculous.

"It's a little weird," I admit. "I guess it matters more how it feels, right?"

"To you or to someone sitting on your lap?"

My libido flares again, and I order myself not to picture Jade perched on my thighs, her perfect, round bottom cupped in my lap.

Way to go, asshole. Now you've got a tent pole in your Santa pants.

I pray the fake belly hides it as I return my gaze to Jade's. "I wonder if it would feel real to someone touching it," I say.

She seems to hesitate for a second. Then she reaches a hand out and presses her palm into the middle of my gut. I flex my abs instinctively, which is ridiculous considering there's five inches of padding over them. Her hand sinks into the foam, and she holds my gaze with amusement in her eyes.

"Very nice," she says. "Soft. Everyone's going to want to hug you."

She's the only one I want hugging me right now. It's all I can think about, the way she'd feel pressed against me, her hair tickling my nose and her breasts soft against my ribs.

I shove my hands in my back pockets to keep from reaching for her, discovering too late that Santa pants don't have back pockets. My hands skid unhindered down the slippery velvet.

Jade giggles. "Did you just pet your ass?"

I give her a sheepish smile. "Just checking the fit."

She peers at my ass, and I could swear I see hunger in her eyes. There's definite heat when she lifts her gaze to mine again.

"They look great," she says. "Good thing Amber picked the shorter coat."

I remember the conversation I overheard that first day in the paddock. The Studmuffin Santa crack. I suppose I should take offense at being discussed like a piece of meat, but I actually like it. Coming from Jade, anyway. It tells me I'm not the only one distracted by the view here.

"Amber picked the jacket?"

Jade nods, and it's her turn to look sheepish. "She wanted to make sure your ass was properly showcased." She lifts one shoulder in a sort of apology. "Sorry about what I said in the paddock," she says. "That first day you showed up? It was unprofessional, and I apologize."

Considering I've had about a hundred unprofessional thoughts about Jade since I got here, there's no way I'm holding that against her. "It's flattering," I tell her honestly. "Besides, I obviously wasn't hired for my Christmas spirit."

The words come out sounding more bitter than I mean them to, and Jade gives me a curious look. "Why do you say that? You seem perfectly jolly to me." She shrugs. "But I guess I don't know you that well."

This is my out. My opportunity to fake some holiday cheer and put on a happy face. My chance to make some cocky sex joke or do something else to get Jade laughing.

But that's not what comes out of my mouth. "I'm not a huge fan of Christmas. Don't worry, I can fake it for the families."

Jade looks at me like I've just admitted I kick puppies for fun, and I wish like hell I hadn't opened my big mouth. "Really?" she asks. "What's not to love about Christmas?"

I should stop talking now, or make up some bullshit about an aversion to pumpkin pie and tinsel.

"My mom walked out a few weeks before Christmas." I hear the words coming out of my mouth, and I'm pretty sure it's the first time I've said them out loud. "Told my dad she was sick of all the fake holiday bullshit and the forced cheer and the ho-ho-ho. Just walked out the door and didn't come back."

"Oh my God."

I nod and keep going, spurred by the softness in Jade's eyes. "My dad tried to hold it together, but he started drinking like a fish, which didn't help the health problems he was already dealing with, so he had a stroke a month later. He's—uh—not been himself ever since."

"Oh, no." Jade lifts a hand to her mouth, her blue eyes wide. "I had no idea. When was this?"

"Senior year." I shrug and scrub a hand over my chin, raking my knuckles across the sandpaper stubble. "I was old enough to get my own meals and drive myself around and stuff, but I wasn't eighteen yet. Children's Services started sniffing around, so my uncle flew out here. The billionaire with the vanity ranch? He took me in until I finished the school year, and I left town the day after graduation."

She stares at me with sadness in her eyes. Not pity—there's a distinction. It's an empathy that makes me long for one of those hugs she mentioned. My whole body aches for the weight of her arms around me.

"Brandon, I'm so sorry." She shakes her head. "You always seemed like you had such a charmed life. The perfect athlete, the perfect grades, the perfect face, the perfect body—"

She stops herself there, cheeks reddening as she drops her eyes. But those eyes have a mind of their own, and as they move across my chest, her face gets redder. She lifts her gaze to mine again. "Why would you take a job as Santa then?"

It's a damn good question. One I shouldn't answer truthfully if we don't want Jade freaking out about her sister hiring someone to watch over the place. "I had this platoon leader who used to hammer us all the time about facing our weaknesses," I say slowly. "I guess that's it."

Part of it, anyway.

She nods and touches a hand to her throat. "I get that," she says. "That's actually pretty admirable."

She's standing so close I could reach out and stroke her hair if I wanted. I *do* want, but I know that would be creepy. She's the one who mentioned hugging earlier. Would that be crossing a line?

"Jade?"

She looks at me, a noticeable heat still in her eyes. "Yeah?"

"Can I get that hug now?"

She hesitates, and I wonder if I'm taking this too far. If I'm forcing myself on her or pushing for unwelcome contact. I open my mouth to tell her to forget it, but before I can get the words out, Jade steps forward and wraps her arms around my neck.

My neck, not my middle. Not the hug you'd give to an elderly relative, but the other kind. The kind that leaves her face tilted upward, her mouth scant inches from mine.

I slide my arms around her, the damn Santa belly wedging itself between us like a jealous pet. I can't feel all of her, but I can feel enough. Her hair ruffles my nose, and her skin smells like fresh gingerbread. I graze the side of her head with my chin like an affection-starved cat.

Jade gives a soft little sigh and meets my eyes. Our gazes lock, and I know I'm going to kiss her. I know she knows, too, and I hold my breath for as long as I can, giving her the chance to pull away.

She doesn't recoil, and I'm drawn to her like a magnet. My lips find hers, and it's like a bomb going off in my brain. There's a gentle buzz in the back of my head, a sweetness at the tip of my tongue as Jade parts her lips and moves against me.

I deepen the kiss, tunneling my fingers into her hair. I can't get enough of all that silky weight in my hands, so I tug out the rubber band to let those honey waves trickle through my fingers.

She moans and presses tighter against me, fingers raking down my back. I cup her shoulder blades in my palms, curving over those delicate wings before sliding up to brush the sides of her face. I kiss her deeper, thumbs skimming the hollows under her cheekbones as my tongue sweeps over her—

"Hey, Jade, did you put the oats in the—oh, hey. Wow."

We jump apart like we've been electrocuted, both of us breathing hard as we turn to face Jade's sister.

"Amber, hey." Jade grabs for the end of her ponytail, surprised to find her hair loose around her shoulders.

I clear my throat and slip her the rubber band, not sure whether to play it cool or shut the hell up and let her do the talking.

Jade folds her fingers around the band and keeps her eyes on her sister. "Um, I was just—uh, helping Brandon with his suit."

"Some of the knots were stuck," I add helpfully, glancing at Jade to see her face is bright pink.

Amber smirks and folds her arms over her chest. "I see," she says. "So you decided to untie them with your tongue?"

I didn't think it was possible for Jade to turn any redder, but her face now matches the bright crimson Christmas sweater Amber is wearing, minus the stitched holly leaves at the center of her chest.

Jade opens her mouth to say something, but Amber waves her

off. "No, I get it. Those prosthetic Santa bellies are super sexy. I can see why you'd be overcome with lust."

"Look, Amber," Jade says, wiping her palms down the legs of her jeans like she's trying to scrape away evidence of our contact. "It's no big deal. Just—uh—welcoming Brandon to the team, that's all."

Amber grins wider, and she glances from her sister to me and back again. "In that case, remind me to have the camera rolling when you welcome all the elves."

I take a step forward, wanting to run interference if Jade needs me to. But she gives me a small head shake and stares down her sister.

"Was there something you needed?" Jade asks.

"Oh, right—any idea why the south gate is wide open?"

"Seriously?"

"Yep," Amber says. "And Tammy wasn't even in that pen, so we can't blame her this time."

Jade shakes her head, looking incredulous. "That new latch is totally reindeer proof," she says. "There's no way one of them did it."

There's unease in both sisters' eyes, and a niggle of worry makes its way from them to me. I remember what Amber told me about odd things happening at the ranch, and I wonder if I can ask questions without rattling any alarm bells for Jade. "Are they okay?" I ask. "The reindeer, I mean. Did they escape?"

Amber shakes her head. "Reindeer have land fidelity," she says. "They might wander a little, but they don't like straying far from home."

"But most people don't know that," Jade says, exchanging a look with her sister. "Someone who wanted to set them loose might try something like that, thinking they'd all take off."

Amber frowns. "You don't think someone would—"

"I don't know," Jade says. "Remember that nasty email we got from the animal rights group?"

"But that's dumb," Amber says. "Letting reindeer roam free just turns them into cougar dinner or bobcat breakfast or—"

"Or roadkill," Jade adds. "You're preaching to the choir."

"So what should we do?"

Jade frowns. "Keep a closer eye on things, I guess."

Amber's not meeting my eyes, and I suspect I should make my exit before she gives something away. "I should, uh—probably try on the rest of the suit."

Both women glance at me, but neither says anything. I grab the Santa coat off the nail and hustle back into the office, wishing like hell I could hit rewind. I want to go back five minutes to feel Jade in my arms again, to kiss her harder and deeper, maybe in the privacy of the office this time.

I slip inside and close the door behind me, conscious of the hushed voices in the barn. I know I should mind my own business, but I find myself pressing an ear against the door, straining to hear their words.

"I knew it!" Amber hisses. "You always had the hots for him."

"I did not!" Jade snaps, and I go from feeling stunned to disappointed in a span of three seconds.

"You did, too," Amber argues. "That's why you didn't want him working here. And you totally kissed him!"

"Look, it was just a one-time thing, okay?" Jade's voice is a whisper, but it slices right through me. "I don't know what happened, but it's not going to happen again."

I peel my ear off the door, heart thudding in my ears.

She's right, of course. The last thing either of us needs is a messy workplace fling. Especially when Jade's in the dark about my reason for being here. That complicates things, and it can't happen again.

But that doesn't stop me from wanting it to.

CHAPTER 5

JADE

"There you go, Mrs. Ramsay," I coax, gripping the reindeer's halter a little tighter as the older woman steps up with her hand outstretched. "This is Vixen. Do you remember the names of all of Santa's reindeer?"

I hum a few bars of "Rudolph the Red-Nosed Reindeer," something I do whenever I bring a member of the herd to the courtyard outside the Central Oregon Dementia Care Unit. Patients who've long since forgotten their own family members' names will burst into song, reciting every word of their favorite Christmas tune.

Mrs. Ramsay beams and nods to an imaginary beat. "You know Dasher and Dancer and Prancer and Vixen!" She sings. "Comet—it makes your teeth turn greeeeen! Comet—it tastes like gasoline! Comet—it makes you vomit! So try Comet, and vomit, todaaaaaay!"

"Close enough," I tell her, smiling at the caregiver who trails behind her pushing a blank-eyed gentleman in a floppy red Santa hat. The man slumps in his wheelchair like he's sleeping, but his eyes are open and fixed on nothing at all.

"That's it," I say to Mrs. Ramsay. "Just pet her really softly on the cheek. See how she likes that?"

The reindeer snorts, not particularly liking it, but accustomed enough to the petting that she's willing to lower her head for more of it. The older woman smiles and runs a hand over the bottom of Vixen's antlers. "Horny," she says. "My late husband was horny, too."

"All right, Mrs. Ramsay," the caregiver says. "That's enough for now. Let's let some of the other patients have a turn, okay?"

Mrs. Ramsay nods and toddles off, humming "Santa, Baby," as another nurse catches her by the arm and throws me a friendly wave before leading the old woman back into the building.

The remaining nurse pushes the wheelchair forward, bringing the motionless man closer. The tip of his Santa hat slides down over one eye, and the nurse leans down to adjust it.

The reindeer shifts uncertainly.

"It's okay, girl," I soothe, giving a soft tug on her halter so she brings her head down to his level. "Here, try giving her this."

I pull a small Fuji apple out of my pocket and hold it out to the man. He doesn't lift his gaze at all. Just keeps staring ahead, his eyes fixed on some unseen point.

"Mr. Brown isn't really verbal," the caregiver whispers to me. "Stroke."

I nod, knowing from experience that the non-verbal patients can still hear perfectly well. I crouch down to his level and try again. "If you'd like to give her this apple, just hold your palm out flat like this."

I demonstrate for him, and Vixen curls her lips, desperate to taste the treat that's just out of reach. I offer it to her, watching the man's face as the reindeer gobbles the apple. I pull another one from my pocket and offer it to him again.

"I'll tell you a secret, okay?" I whisper to him. "I know her nose band says Vixen, but her real name is Irene. Vixen's just a stage name, but don't tell anyone, okay?"

There's a flicker of something in the man's eyes. Just a faint ghost of something that dances across those cloudy brown irises before flitting away. I hold the second apple closer, waiting for him to take it.

"You want to try, or should I give it to her for you?" I ask.

The man doesn't lift either hand, but there's a faint tilt to his head. A nod toward me, so I palm the apple and hold it out to the reindeer. She gobbles it with relish, munching and smacking and slobbering a little on the man's pant leg.

This time, I'm certain one corner of his mouth tips up. The other side stays lifeless, but I sense this is the closest we'll get to an actual smile. I stand up and wipe my hands on my pants.

"Thank you," the caregiver murmurs to me as she backs up the wheelchair. "Mr. Brown, are you ready for lunch now?"

The man doesn't say anything, but as the caregiver steers him away, his fingers flutter ever so slightly in my direction. I watch them disappear into the building, a faint breeze lifting the man's wispy white hair like a wing.

"Jade?"

I turn to see Brandon Brown approaching from the parking lot. He looks at me, then back toward the building where the man in the wheelchair has just disappeared. "What are you doing here?" he asks.

Irene snorts, saving me the trouble of making a smartass comment. "Introducing reindeer to patients," I tell him, wishing my stupid heart didn't race at the sight of him. "Why are you here?"

His eyes cloud just a little, and he tilts his head toward the door. "That's my dad," he says. "The guy in the wheelchair."

There's a roaring in my ears, and it takes me a few seconds to process what he just said. "Your dad? The one who had the—oh, Brandon. I'm so sorry."

"Thank you." He nods and shifts his weight from one foot to the other. "I've had a long time to get used to it."

"That must be difficult," I tell him. "Seeing your dad like that."

"Yeah. He has good days and bad days. More bad days than good, lately. That's actually why I came home."

"Is he—" I'm not sure how to ask the question, but Brandon nods without me needing to say another word.

"Yes," he says. "The doctors say his kidneys are failing. That he doesn't have much longer. That seemed like my cue to get back here."

"Are you really thinking of leaving the service?"

He shrugs. "I've considered it. Or maybe just leaving active duty. There's a job opening at the local recruitment office in a couple months. That's one way I could stay in while sticking close to home."

"I hope it works out for you."

The job, I mean. His dad won't be getting any better. I can tell from the dullness in Brandon's eyes, and I want to wrap my arms around him and pat his back. That strong, muscular, tattooed back. Instead, I tighten my grip on Irene's lead rope. "If it makes you feel better, I think he really liked the reindeer," I tell him. "We even got a smile out of him."

"My dad smiled?" Brandon's voice is so incredulous that, for a moment, I wonder if I imagined the whole thing. "That's—wow, that doesn't happen much."

"If you want, I can give you the schedule," I offer. "I just started bringing the reindeer out here last month, and a lot of the patients are really into it."

He nods and shoves his hands in his pockets. "My dad always loved animals. He used to love Christmas, but it kind of lost its luster after—well, after."

His voice is heavy as a lead ball, and Irene shuffles her hooves. I'm torn between feeling sorry for Brandon and remembering that kiss. A one-time thing, obviously. Not something either of us plans to repeat.

"You'd better get in there," I tell him. "They were just taking him to lunch, so maybe you can sit with him."

"Good idea," he says. "Will I see you tomorrow night for the photo shoot?"

I shake my head. "I have other plans, but you guys don't need me. Amber's running the show, and the photographer is someone we went to school with, so you'll be in good hands."

"Sounds like she has big plans for the website and marketing."

"That's the idea." I smile. "My sister's pretty talented."

"So are you," he says. "I'm impressed with what you guys are doing out there."

"Thanks." I try not to let the big, dorky smile take over my face, but I'm not sure I'm succeeding.

"So I'll see you out there on opening day."

"Yep," I agree, running my hand down Irene's cheek. "Looking forward to it."

As I watch Brandon walk away, I'm annoyed to realize how very true that is.

CHAPTER 6

BRANDON

On a scale of one to ten, how big of an asshole am I for hiding out in the men's room until I'm sure my dad has finished lunch?

It's not that I'm not eager to see him. I missed him like hell every time I shipped out, and visiting him has been my first stop anytime a tour ended.

But watching him eat—watching a nurse spoon mashed potatoes into the mouth of a guy who used to feed me baby food—is more than I can bear. This strong ox of a man who came to all my football games and used to heft our family Christmas tree overhead like he was pressing a barbell has been reduced to someone who can't lift a spoon by himself.

I owe him the dignity of not having me watch him eat.

"Hey, Pop," I greet as I walk into his room after lunch.

He doesn't look up. Just stares out the window at the garden that last night's frost has left shriveled and brown.

I take my seat beside him anyway and rest a hand on his knee. His eyes stay fixed on some unseen point outside, or maybe on nothing at all. He's wearing a pudding-stained T-shirt and a

Santa hat with a pom-pom that flops over one eye. He doesn't seem to notice the obstruction.

The indignity of it all makes my chest hurt.

"Here, let me take that off you." I yank off the Santa hat, irritated by everything he's had to suffer through. Divorce isn't fair. Having a stroke at fifty-one isn't fair. At least I can save the guy the humiliation of looking like Insane Asylum Santa.

My father drags his gaze off the garden and studies me as I set the hat on top of his dresser. Beside it is a framed photo of me in my dress blues the day I was awarded the Medal of Honor. A lump forms in my throat, and I wonder how much my dad understands about what I've been doing these last thirteen years. Somewhere in there, does he know I'm his son?

"Let me clean that off for you," I tell him. I grab the photo by the edge of the frame and use the hem of my T-shirt to polish the glass. "There," I say, setting it back on the dresser. "Good as new."

There's another photo beside it, a grainy one of my youthful-looking father holding a blue-swaddled bundle in the hospital delivery room. It's the first photo of the two of us together, and I have no idea how it got here.

"That's a good picture of you," I tell him, for lack of anything better to say.

My dad doesn't respond.

Rage pools sour in my gut as I think about the day my mother walked out. Fucking Frosty the Snowman was playing on the stereo, its tinny-sounding cheer an ironic backdrop to the words my mother shouted.

"I'm fed up to here with this Christmas crap!

I can't handle this.

This isn't what I signed on for."

My dad just sat there on the couch with a bottle of beer in one hand and a dumbstruck look on his face.

He was wearing a goddamn Santa hat then, too.

I shake off the memory and try to think of something calming to talk about.

"I've been working out at Uncle Cort's ranch," I say. I stop there, not sure if he has any clue Cort is dead and his kids have taken it over. I haven't said anything, but I don't know if my cousins have visited or what they've said about their dad's passing.

"I've been doing a lot of woodworking out there," I continue, feeling idiotic for carrying on like this to a guy who probably doesn't have a clue what I'm saying. I'm never sure how much he understands. "And I've been doing some part-time stuff at a reindeer ranch."

Still no response, though his gaze flicks once over the Santa hat on the dresser. Coincidence, or is he following along?

I wonder if thoughts of Christmas past fill him with the same sort of fury they give me, or if it's all blank in there. I'd almost prefer the latter. Not remembering at all, not having to think about my mother's Christmas tirade.

I haven't seen her since that day, though I heard through the grapevine she lives in Florida somewhere.

"There's this girl named Jade I really like a lot."

I have no idea why I just said that. Yeah, we kissed, but I've kissed plenty of women.

Not women like her.

"Anyway, she's been teaching me stuff about reindeer. Did you know both male and female reindeer grow antlers? They're the only deer species that does that. And they lose their antlers every winter."

Still no response from my dad, so I keep blathering like a dumbass. "They have this tendon thing in their ankles that rubs over the bone and makes a clicking sound," I continue. "It's how they find each other when they're walking around in the dark or in bad weather."

Slowly my dad turns his head and goes back to staring out the window. A lump thickens in my throat, and I wonder if he'll even recall I was here by the time he goes to bed tonight.

I don't know how long we sit there in silence like that. Eventually, I take my hand off his knee and get awkwardly to my feet. "I'm going to get going now, okay? It was good seeing you, Pop."

He keeps staring out the window. I bend down and give him a stiff sort of side hug. He doesn't hug back, but he does lean into me just a little. That's something.

By the time I get to my truck, there's a hollow pit in my stomach. Or maybe I'm just hungry, since I skipped lunch to come here. I drive to the burger joint over by the high school. My teammates and I used to hang out there after football practice, fueling up for the next big game.

I'm not surprised when I walk in and spot a whole pack of them in the corner.

"Hey, Brown! Over here."

I make my way toward the booth in the corner, which is filled with faces I recognize. Jimmy Albrich. Brian Grimes. A few girls I used to know whose names are escaping me at the moment.

I sit down on the edge of a bench seat and find myself across from one girl whose name I do remember.

"Hey, Bran. Good to see you again." Stacey Fleming reaches across the table and touches my hand, and I can't decide whether I'm happy or edgy about it. "You still hanging out at the reindeer place?"

"Yeah," I answer, directing my response at the whole table. "It's shaping up to be pretty cool. Tell everyone you know to bring their kids out when it opens."

"We'll do that." Another girl whose name I don't remember edges closer to me on the bench seat. That earns her a glare from Stacey, who hasn't let go of my hand yet.

"That Jade chick sure got hot."

I whip my head around to see who said it. Chris Renner,

varsity runningback my senior year. He was always kind of an asshole, so I don't feel bad about the dirty look I shoot him.

"I don't remember her from high school," I admit. "But she seems like a great girl."

"Great rack, that's for sure," Chris says as he stuffs a handful of fries in his mouth. The comment prompts a round of laughter from the guys at the table, and an uneasy glance between the women.

I fix Chris with my iciest stare. The one a former drill sergeant once dubbed "the death glare."

"Don't be an asshole, Renner," I snap. "That's fucking disrespectful, and you know it."

He has the good grace to look embarrassed. "Sorry, man," he mutters. "I didn't know you and Miss P—uh, that you and Jade were a thing."

I open my mouth to correct his misguided assumption that I'd only defend a woman I'm sleeping with, but I stop myself. I don't owe any of these people an explanation.

"I think she's sweet." That comment comes from a girl at the far end of the table whose name is either Heather or Holly. I'm not positive. "And she's done really well for herself out there."

Stacey gives a grudging nod and strokes a finger over the ridge of my knuckles. "She sure has," Stacey says. "Hopefully you won't be spending all your time out there, Bran. We'd sure love to see more of you, now that you're back in town."

I clear my throat and nod. "Yeah. Look, I'm gonna go grab some food. Anyone want anything?"

Everyone shakes their heads as I stand up and turn toward the smell of grilled meat. I feel eyes on my back as I make my way to the front counter, and I'm not sure whose they are. Maybe all of them.

There's a weird feeling in my gut that I'm pretty sure has nothing to do with hunger.

* * *

I TAKE the long way back home, telling myself I'm just enjoying a scenic tour of all my old hometown haunts.

But there's only one reason for me to pass by the Central Oregon Dementia Care Unit at this hour, and it has nothing to do with my dad. I'm hoping for a glimpse of Jade, just a peek of her visiting with patients or loading up the reindeer.

What I don't expect is the sight I see as I pull through the parking lot.

"Everything okay?" I call as I roll down my window and draw up close.

She looks up from where she's peering under the hood of a beat-up work truck and frowns at me. "I think the battery's dead. Which is stupid, since it's brand new."

"You leave your lights on or something?"

"Definitely not." Her frown deepens. "Not today, anyway. I've had a couple mornings lately where I've come out to find the lights on and the battery dead. Maybe I'm more distracted than I thought."

I don't want to say it, but that's one of the things Amber mentioned when she talked about odd happenings at the ranch. "Maybe it's worth locking the truck at night," I suggest. "Just to be safe."

Jade sighs. "It's a freakin' ranch in the middle of nowhere Oregon," she says. "No one locks their doors."

"Humor me."

Jade looks at the battery again, then back at me. "I don't suppose I could talk you into jumping me?"

My libido lunges, and it's on the tip of my tongue to say something inappropriate. But that's not what she needs right now.

"Got jumper cables?" I ask as I put the truck in park and ease out the door.

"Yeah," she says. "I'll go grab them."

She runs around the side of the truck, giving me a chance to check out her ass as well as the impressive rig hooked to the back of the truck. It's like a retro-fitted horse trailer, and I see two pairs of antlers moving around inside. I step closer and slip two fingers through the slats near the front.

"Hey, guys," I murmur as I stroke a downy nose. "You keeping warm back there?"

Footsteps behind me signal Jade's return, and I pivot to see her already hooking the red clamp to her battery. "Thanks so much," she says as she offers me the other end of the cables. "Getting stuck out here with a pair of hungry reindeer isn't my idea of a good time. Or theirs."

"No prob." I shuffle around to the front of my truck and pop the hood, taking a second to flick a speck of corrosion off the battery. "Why don't you get in my truck where it's warm?" I offer. "No sense standing out here freezing your butt off."

I expect her to argue, to insist she's just fine where she is. To my surprise, she nods. "Thanks," she says. "That's a good idea."

She turns and walks around to the other side of my truck while I finish hooking the black clamp to the metal strut propping the hood open. Then I pop open the driver's side door and slide behind the wheel. There's a faint smell of gingerbread filling the cab, and Jade gives me a small smile.

"Thanks again," she says. "I'm not used to being rescued like this."

"You can quit thanking me, Jade. You'd do the same thing for anyone else."

I turn over the engine, firing it to a low roar as the heaters kick on and blast us with a warm gust of air. The stereo blares to life with a screeching country song, and I reach across her to turn it off.

She smiles again. "Were you coming by to see your dad again?"

I should probably say yes. It's the simplest explanation.

But it's not the one I offer. "No. I was hoping you'd still be here."

"Me?"

I nod. "I wanted to make sure you got home okay."

She scoffs a little at that, stretching her legs out across the floorboards in front of her. "You don't have to watch out for me, Brandon. I'm a big girl."

"Everyone needs someone watching out for them," I tell her. "Learned that in the Marines."

Her expression softens a bit. "I guess I'm in good company, then."

"You'd make a badass Field Artillery Officer."

"Thanks. I think."

We're silent for a few beats, listening to the soft hum of the engine and the rush of wind hurling crackly leaf carcasses against the window.

When Jade speaks again, her voice is soft. "I—uh—should probably apologize for what happened in the barn the other day."

I turn to look at her. "You mean the kiss?"

She nods, and it's all I can do not to roll my eyes. "I'm a consenting adult, Jade. I kissed you because I wanted to kiss you."

Her eyes jerk to mine, and she frowns again. "*I* kissed *you*," she says. "Which I totally shouldn't have done as your boss."

"You're not my boss," I retort, well aware that I sound like a misbehaving ten-year-old. "Amber oversees me, and besides that, *I* kissed *you*."

"You did not," she snaps. "I totally put the moves on you like some kind of floozy."

"What the hell are you talking about?" I demand, irritation growing. "I distinctly remember mashing my lips against yours and macking on you like a creeper, and I'm sorry if I took advantage."

"Took advantage?" She snort-laughs, and I'd probably find it adorable if she didn't look like she wants to punch me. "No one takes advantage of me, I can tell you that much. And I'm absolutely positive *I'm* the one who kissed *you,* which is why I'm trying to apologize for—"

"You know what? This is stupid. Let's settle it right now."

"How are you going to—*oh*—"

Whatever she was going to say is smothered by my lips pressing against hers. I half expect her to bite me or push me away, but her response is the opposite. She grabs the front of my coat and yanks me closer, kissing me back with a fierceness that steals my breath.

I respond in kind, damn sure there will be no question of who's kissing whom. I've never wanted to kiss anyone the way I want to kiss Jade, so I thread my fingers into her hair and brush her tongue with mine.

She lets go of my coat and shoves her hands inside, palms kneading my chest through the nubby wool sweater I'm wearing. Her touch is rough and hungry, and I find myself needing to touch her, too. I let go of the steering wheel and tug at the zipper on her coat, braced for her to resist.

But she presses closer, shifting so her flannel-covered breast slides into my hand like the best damn Christmas gift I've ever gotten. Jesus, she's soft. So soft, which is the opposite of how we're kissing right now. There's a frantic energy to it, a feeling of wanting to devour each other.

Jade slides her hand down and yanks the hem of my T-shirt from my jeans. Her eager fingers burrow beneath the layers, tunneling up and over my bare chest. I stifle a groan and take my cue from her, praying my hand isn't cold as I slip it under her shirt. She gasps, but not with discomfort. That's clear the instant I skim a thumb over her peaked nipple, and she cries out in response.

"God, yes. Oh, please, Brandon."

"Jade," I murmur against her mouth.

"More."

Her breast fills my hand, and our breath fills the cab of the truck, steaming the driver's side window. I can't get enough of her, and I'm drowning in all this heat and friction and energy and—

"What the hell?" she says.

I jerk back as Jade pulls away and blinks.

"I'm sorry," I tell her. "I got carried away with—"

"Not you," she says, scrambling across the bench seat to yank at the door handle. "Oh my God, my truck!"

She's out the door and on the ground running before I can figure out what the hell just happened. It takes me a second to process the fact that Jade is standing beside the driver's side door of her pickup, shirt untucked, as she shouts at a cotton-haired woman in a nightgown. The old lady grips the steering wheel like a life buoy, so short she's forced to peer through the middle.

I push open my own truck door and jump out, halfway to Jade's side before the door of the clinic opens, and a nurse comes rushing out. "Mrs. Peterson! Stop! Oh my God—"

"I'm goin' for a joyride!" hoots the little old lady with an impressive set of pipes. She grips the wheel in both hands and revs the engine as Jade and the nurse try unsuccessfully to pry her out of the cab.

"Mrs. Peterson, please stop," the nurse urges.

It takes all three of us to wrangle one elflike senior citizen who couldn't weigh more than ninety pounds soaking wet. We're all breathing hard by the time we get her out of the cab. Her feet are bare, so I hold her in my arms as she flails and kicks and shouts something about missing the Buddy Holly concert.

"Goddamnn cops," she growls as she whacks my chest with a gnarled fist. "I'm sixteen years old, and I have my license, and Daddy said I could take the Camaro."

"I'm so sorry," the nurse pants, and I'm not sure if she's talking to me, Jade, or Mrs. Peterson. "Someone left the side door unlocked. We've had problems before with her trying to steal cars, but I didn't think—"

"It's fine," Jade says, glancing at me. "No harm done. Everything's good with my truck now, so I'll just get out of here."

I start to protest, desperate to find some way to continue what Jade and I started back there in my truck. But that's tough to do with my arms full of feisty octogenarian, so instead I nod. "I'll, uh—see you at the ranch?"

She nods and skirts past me to unhook the jumper cables, moving like a bank robber prepping the getaway car. "Sure," she says, her voice a little breathless. "See you at the ranch."

I hardly have time to step back before she's revving the engine and peeling out of the parking lot, reindeer peering back at me from the trailer with bewildered looks on their faces.

CHAPTER 7

JADE

"Ho, ho, ho!"

Brandon's voice booms like a kettle drum, and the woman hovering at his side quivers to its rhythm. Touching a hand to her ample cleavage, she offers him either an eye-twitch or a lash-flutter. It's tough to tell with Blitzen's antlers blocking my view.

"What did you just call me?" The woman's tone is coquettish, and the way she leans across Brandon's arm to adjust her toddler on his lap ensures optimum contact between her boob and his bicep.

Amber leans in to whisper in my ear. "Is that the sixth or seventh time he's heard that stupid 'ho ho ho' line today?"

I shrug and pretend not to care as I survey the impressive line leading all the way to the back of the barn. "I'm guessing it won't be the last time."

"He's handling it like a champ," Amber says. "Not lapping it up, but not being a dick about it, either."

"Is this where you ask me to pat you on the back?" I mutter.

My sister grins and turns on her heel to present me with her shoulders. I whack them a little harder than necessary, earning myself a squeak of protest. "Hey!" she says. "Can I help it if I'm a marketing genius for hiring a Santa who can handle women fawning over him?"

Her words send a flash of embarrassment through me, mostly because I was one of those women fawning over him last week.

But seven days is plenty of time to move past our accidental lip lock—okay, two lip locks—and Brandon and I have been consummate professionals since then. It's like we've both forgotten those kisses ever happened.

The hell you have. There's no forgetting kissing like that.

My sister turns back around, and I thrust a curry comb into her hands. "Here," I tell her. "That family in the matching sweaters paid the extra fifty bucks for reindeer grooming. Cupid should be up for it."

She nods and hustles away, while I move to the other side of the pen where a toddler is making a valiant attempt to hand his baby brother's teething ring to a shaggy blonde reindeer. Blitzen's antlers poke through the bars, earning a squeal of delight from the kid.

"Is that your mom over there?" I ask, nodding to yet another flirty young woman bending low in front of Brandon to show him the blinking Christmas light necklace nestled in her cleavage.

The kid nods and draws back the rattle. "Yeah. She said she's gonna have a special talk with Santa to make sure we all get what we want for Christmas."

"I'm sure she did." I reach down and pry the kid's chubby fingers off the bars as Blitzen snuffles at the teething ring. "Let's find a better snack for him, okay?"

I fish into my pocket for a handful of the rolled corn I filled it with an hour ago, surprised to find I'm down to just a few kernels. It's been a busy day of wheedling with kids and moms who've lined up since eight-o'clock this morning to see the reindeer.

Oh, who am I kidding?

They're here to see Studmuffin Santa, and I can't say I blame them.

"Ho, ho, ho!" His jolly bellow pings off the rafters, and I remember what he told me about his less-than-happy Christmas memories. I think about his dad at the care center and wonder what it would be like to have that sort of dark cloud hanging over Christmas. How did I not know about his parents? It's a medium-sized town, and gossip spreads fast here.

People only hear what they want to when it comes to the hometown hero.

"Here you go," I tell the kid at my feet. "Offer it to him nice and gentle, with your hand out flat like this."

He does as instructed, giggling when Blitzen's velvety lips flap against his palm as he takes the proffered treat.

"She kissed me!"

Blitzen paws the ground, irritated more by the vanishing corn than the incorrect gender pronoun. At the edge of the pen, my sister's ex-boyfriend clicks his camera shutter and gives me a thumbs up. Then he turns around to snag a shot of a family that's waited in line an hour to see the reindeer.

He looks up as my sister walks past and gives the same puppy dog look he's worn every time they've split up. "Hey, Amber, what are you doing after work?"

My sister shoots me a pleading look, and I do my best to save her. "Remember we were going to give Blitzen a bath?"

Amber nods and turns back to Zak. "I'm pretty busy on the ranch these days, you know?"

Zak gives her an earnest look, dark hair flopping over his eye. "There's more to life than work, you know."

"Not right now, there's not," she says. "This is what I need to be doing."

He shrugs and draws the camera back to his eye. "Maybe another time."

My sister moves to a spot halfway between the reindeer pen and Santa's throne and cups her hands around her mouth like a megaphone. "We have about thirty minutes until closing time," she calls out, earning a groan from some of the families at the back of the line. "Santa's going to make sure he sees all of you, but we're going to have to close the doors so we don't have more people lining up."

I step closer to her and do my own version of megaphone mouth. "That's right, we have to let Santa get back to the North Pole tonight so he can make sure the elves are getting all your toys built."

"Tell all your friends," Amber adds. "Santa's here Tuesday through Sunday until December twenty-fourth."

I feel Brandon's eyes on me, even though I'm not looking at him. Even though I've done my damnedest not to look at him any more than necessary. That hasn't stopped me from thinking about the kisses in the barn or the groping in his truck. What would have happened if Amber hadn't walked in or if the old lady hadn't tried to carjack me?

"I almost forgot," Amber says, tugging my ponytail as she steps around me to empty a box of mini candy canes into a red bowl. "I put some cookies on your desk. You should offer some to Studmuffin Santa when his shift is done. I don't think he got lunch today."

"Hmph," is the most intelligent response I can muster. I steal a glance at Brandon, not surprised to see a pair of doe-eyed twenty-somethings arranging themselves on each of his knees while Zak gamely shoots photos.

"You don't mind, do you?" coos the brunette on his left knee as she twines her arms around his neck. "It's just that we've been such good girls this year."

The blonde on his right knee giggles and puts a hand on his chest. "Now that we're both on your lap, maybe we can talk about the first thing that pops up."

I roll my eyes and turn back to my sister. "Is that three times or four for that line?"

"At this point, I'm just counting the number of times I gag."

"Come on," I say. "Help me swap out Comet for the last thirty minutes. Prancer needs more practice tolerating all the squealing."

"If he figures out the secret, tell him to share it with the rest of us."

Amber and I work together to make the switch, herding Comet back out into the pasture and ushering in a festive-looking Prancer to oohs and ahhs from kids. The bells jingle on his harness, and I'm so busy doing my job that I almost forget about Brandon.

Almost. I glance back to see him chatting with one of the rare dads in the bunch, someone I recognize as one of Brandon's old teammates. The guys are laughing and smiling, but Brandon keeps his focus on the guy's kid, never breaking character as Santa.

"He really does have a knack for it," I admit.

Amber gives me a knowing look. "I told you he'd be perfect."

Too perfect for you, my subconscious chides.

"I need to work on the permit applications for some of the traveling events," I tell her. "Do you have everything handled out here for now?"

"No problem," she says. "I promised the elves extra cookies if they stick around and help with cleanup."

"You're the best."

I steal one more look at Brandon before heading off to the office and shutting the door behind me.

For the next hour, I lose myself in paperwork. Raising and traveling with reindeer is a highly-regulated business, with a constant flood of forms and permits for the Oregon Department of Fish and Wildlife. I'm meticulously organized with them, which is why I'm annoyed I can't find a stack of health certificates I'm positive I left on the edge of my desk.

I paw through the file cabinet one more time, slamming the door shut with more force than necessary when the forms don't turn up.

"Everything okay?"

I jump at the sound of Brandon's voice. "Jesus, you scared me."

"Sorry," he says from the doorway. "I knocked before I opened it, but you must not have heard me."

"It's fine, come on in."

His face is bare, which is jarring after nine hours of seeing him in a Santa beard. He's stuffed the fake facial hair into his Santa hat, which he's holding in one hand. His cheeks are ruddy, and there's a shadow of stubble on his chin.

He looks ridiculously hot, and I hate that I notice.

"Did the lines finally clear out?" I ask.

"Yeah. That private investigator dude who did my background check showed up at the last second with his niece, so Amber let him in."

"I'm sure Zak loved that."

"The photographer?"

"Yep. Amber's ex-boyfriend who isn't quite over her."

"That's right, you mentioned that," he says. "And the PI has the hots for her?"

"Bingo," I say. "Well, him and everyone else."

He smiles. "She's a sweet kid."

I nod, not disagreeing with him. But since every man with a pulse seems to fall for my beautiful younger sister, I'm surprised he'd describe her that way.

Brandon shifts the Santa hat from one hand to the other. "You feel like things went well today?"

"Yeah," I say. "We had twice the visitor volume I expected, so that was great." I pause, catching sight of the smudges on his face. "Nice lipstick."

Brandon lifts a hand to his face where lip prints ranging from rose to plum line his cheekbone like bizarre tribal tattoos. He starts to scrub at them with the sleeve of his Santa suit, but I grab a box of Kleenex off my desk and shove them at him.

"Here. Don't get it all over the coat."

"Thanks." Brandon grabs two tissues and swipes at his face, totally missing the biggest smattering of kiss marks near his temple.

I watch him keep trying, knowing damn well I should point him toward the bathroom so he can look in a mirror and do this himself. But some stupid part of me can't resist the excuse to touch him again.

"Here, let me help." I grab another tissue from the box and stretch up to dab at a smudge of sticky peach gloss near his hairline.

"Thanks," he says, turning his head as I put two fingers to his chin to nudge him the other way. "You knew it would be like this, didn't you?"

I know what he's talking about. The flirting, the attention, the fact that women—present company included—can't keep their hands off him.

I swipe at a stubborn blotch of crimson below his right eye. "Yes," I admit, the lone syllable coming out huskier than I want it to. "I had a feeling. Did you?"

His eyes lock with mine, and my breath catches in my throat.

"I thought it might happen," he murmurs.

His skin is warm under my fingers, and I can't seem to tear my gaze off his. I finally manage it, but only make it as far as his mouth. I linger there, remembering how those lips felt against mine. It takes every ounce of self-control I have not to kiss him.

I clear my throat. "It can't be a huge hardship to have women throwing themselves at you all day." My words sound snarkier than I mean them to, and I'm surprised to see his brows furrow. I drop my hands from his face and look at him. "Is it?"

He shrugs again. "It's kind of a dick move to complain about female attention."

"That didn't answer my question."

He stares right into my eyes, and I order myself not to look away. "You didn't answer mine, either."

"I've forgotten what it was."

"I asked if everything was okay."

"Oh." I wave a dismissive hand. "It's fine. Just some missing paperwork, no biggie."

"I see." He quirks an eyebrow at me. "So you weren't in here slamming drawers because you were overcome with jealousy at the sight of all those women pawing me?"

I snort. "Hardly. I barely noticed."

That's such a blatant lie that neither of us bothers saying anything else. I crumple the tissue in my hand, but I don't step back. I glance at the wall, my gaze landing on a photo of Amber and me posing with our arms around Donner. It was taken just after this whole crazy Christmas plan started to take root, and we were brimming with hope and happiness and ideas for how to make the business succeed.

Brandon clears his throat. "To answer your question, yes—it's awkward."

I swing my gaze back to him, surprised to realize he's still focused on the question. "Do you want to quit?" I ask, surprised at the flutter of worry in my belly.

He shakes his head and gives me a small smile that doesn't quite reach his eyes. "I don't. Like I said, a guy's not supposed to complain about shit like that."

"But?"

He looks at me for a long moment, like he's deciding whether to say something. "I feel bad for the husbands," he says. "The guys sitting at home with their thumbs up their asses watching football while their wives grope some stranger in a red velvet suit."

I nod, wondering how much of this has to do with his

parents. With his mom walking out. "In the grand scheme of things, it's better than going out to a strip club or looking at porn, isn't it?"

I'm not sure that's the right comparison to make, or if it even is better. But I know I'm feeling unexpectedly sorry for Brandon.

"So it's a choice between collecting a porn stash or groping a childhood icon in front of your kid?" He sighs and leans back against my office wall, a smudge of missed glitter-gloss twinkling at the edge of his eyebrow. "Never mind, I'm just being a dick. And yeah, I know there were plenty of women today without husbands or boyfriends or anything. Women free to grope anyone they want to grope."

When he puts it that way, I feel kind of crummy about the whole thing. About treating Brandon like a sex object. "Look, I don't want you to feel like a piece of meat."

"Studmuffin Santa?" There's that wistful smile again. "It's fine. It's only for a few weeks, right?"

"Right." And that's my reminder. Whatever happened between Brandon and me last week was a temporary thing, and I need to remember that.

My gaze drops to his mouth, and I forget all over again. Or rather, I remember what it felt like to kiss him. The softness of his lips, the roughness of his hands in my hair, and a faint taste of cinnamon candy.

"Gingerbread," I blurt, turning away in desperate need of distraction. "I almost forgot, my sister made cookies. Help yourself."

I hustle around to the other side of my desk, hopeful a piece of furniture between us will quell my desire to touch him. Brandon's eyes widen as he takes in the big plate of cookies, and he sits down in the chair on the other side of the desk.

"Wow, thanks," he says. "I haven't eaten all day."

"Sorry," I say, feeling guilty again. "If you want, I can run up to the house and heat up a freezer burrito or something."

"Nah, it's my own fault. My cousin made me a sandwich this morning, but I forgot to bring it. These look good, though."

He reaches for the plate of cookies and picks one up by the leg. Too late, he discovers it's two gingerbread figures melded together in a compromising position.

"Well, that's interesting." He holds it up for a better look, and I grimace at the sight of one fat-headed gingerbread man with its face wedged between the thighs of another.

"Accidental pastry porn," I say, determined not to blush this time. "Probably got placed too close together on the baking sheet." I pick up a cookie of my own and frown at it. "Or not an accident."

Brandon takes the cookie from my hand and inspects it. "Where did you say these came from?"

I study another gingerbread figure that boasts an impressive set of breasts fashioned out of red hots and slightly melted Hersey's kisses. "Dammit, Amber."

"The pubic hair is a nice touch," Brandon points out as he hands back my cookie. "I've never seen toasted coconut used quite like that."

"My sister, the comedienne." I start to put the cookie back, but decide better of it. I take a bite, savoring the spicy sweetness. "She's lucky I didn't take these out there to share with kids."

"You two are pretty close?"

"Yeah," I admit, leaning back in my chair and wishing I had some milk. "We're a good team. She's the marketing whiz, and I know animals."

"You've got a degree in veterinary medicine?"

I take another bite of cookie, not bothering to mask my surprise. "How did you know that?"

"It's on your website," he says. "That's a great picture of you, by the way."

"What picture?" I don't wait for a response. I set down my cookie and jiggle the mouse to wake my computer, then punch in the URL for Jingle Bell Reindeer Ranch. "She said she had a surprise for me, but I didn't realize she'd already finished."

"It looks great," Brandon says. "The picture is under 'about us' or 'meet the staff' or something like that."

I toggle my way to the page, admiring my sister's design skills. The layout is simple but professional, with a smattering of reindeer hoof prints across the top of each page. "I didn't know she'd finished it," I say. "She's been working on it for months, but I thought we still had the old site up."

"This one is a lot cooler," he says. "I saw the old one when I applied for the job, but this one's more user-friendly."

"It's awesome." I flip to the photo of me at the bottom of the screen and stop. It's a candid shot that Amber took last summer when the weather was hot and the new calves were just getting their antlers. I'm in shorts and a black tank top leaning over Marcus—stage name Dancer—giving him a kiss on his fuzzy reindeer face. My hair is in my eyes, and I'm laughing at his attempt to lick my cheek.

I glance up to see Brandon looking at me.

"You're really beautiful," he says softly, "but you know what makes you even hotter?"

I shake my head, too surprised by the website and by Brandon's compliment to come up with a smartass reply. "No."

"The fact that you don't have a clue."

I bite my lip. "Did you just call me clueless?"

"I'm saying you're gorgeous, and you don't know it. That's hot as hell. You're not full of yourself."

"Thanks. I think." I nod once, not sure how else to respond. It's not the first time I've been complimented, but it's the first time I've heard it from someone who looks like Brandon Brown. Someone whose lips I haven't stopped feeling for a week.

"Thanks," I say again, averting my eyes. "Let's see what else she put on the website." My cheeks prickle with heat, and I'm not sure why I feel so undone. I focus on flipping through the tabs.

Event calendar.

Reindeer games.

Real country weddings.

Get in touch.

I click the contact link, hoping she remembered the coded email form we talked about.

Tinny electric guitar music blasts from my speakers.

Bow-chicka-bow-wow!

"What the—"

"Oh my God." Brandon jerks up and jabs a finger at the screen. "That's a scene from *I Cream on Jeanie*."

"What is it doing on my website?" I shriek.

"I don't know, but there's a part coming up here where she takes the maple syrup and—"

"Ew, stop!" I yelp, not sure if I'm talking to Brandon or the computer. "How the hell do I get this off my website?"

Brandon stands up and reaches for the mouse, making a vain attempt to mute it. The music keeps blaring. "A better question is why it's on your website in the first place."

That is a better question, so yank my phone out of my pocket and hit speed dial for Amber.

"Yo!" She answers on the first ring. "Jeez, turn down that godawful music. And who's moaning?"

"That's what I'd like to know." I look back at the screen and immediately wish I hadn't. "Why is there porn on our website?"

"What?" There's a rustling on the other end of the line, followed by the clack of computer keys. "Where? What are you talking about?"

"It's on the 'Get in touch,' page." I wait while she scrambles to get there.

Brandon continues tapping at the keys, finally silencing the moans.

"Thank you," I whisper.

"Who are you thanking?" Amber asks. "And what on earth—oh my God, I can't unsee that."

Brandon frowns at the screen. "Maybe you should look away," he whispers. "This next part with the pacifier is a little—uh—graphic."

"Why do you know this movie by heart?" I hiss.

He grimaces. "A guy in my barracks had a serious porn habit. Believe me, I tried not to watch."

"Is that Brandon?" Amber asks. "You're watching porn with Brandon?"

"No, I'm not watching porn with Brandon," I snap. "Not on purpose anyway. How the hell do we fix this? If someone's kid clicks on our page—"

"I know, I know, I'm on it," Amber interrupts. "Okay, I just disabled the page. Hit refresh and tell me it's gone."

I do what she says, more relieved than I've ever been to see a 404 error message. "It's gone," I tell her. "How did it get there in the first place?"

"I have no idea," she says. "I put the finishing touches on it last night and was waiting to surprise you with it after everyone went home."

"I couldn't be more surprised if Dasher knocked on the front door and asked for Grey Poupon."

"Jade, you have to know I didn't do this on purpose."

"I know, hon." My sister may be the bake-risque-gingerbread-man kind of perv, but she's not a post-porn-on-a-family-website kind of perv.

It's a fine distinction.

"The site looks great," I assure her. "Besides the porn, I mean."

"Look, I don't have a clue how this happened, but I'll figure it out," Amber says. "In the meantime, I'll change all the passwords and have the real page up again in ten minutes. You can check it out then, okay?"

"Okay." I glance at Brandon, who's watching me oddly. "Thanks for taking care of that. And thanks for the surprise."

"Porn aside."

"It was educational."

I click to end the call and turn back to Brandon. "I guess I owe you some big thanks."

"For what?"

"I never would have discovered that if you hadn't told me to check out the website."

"That porn wasn't there last night," he says. "I definitely would have noticed."

I sigh and shove back from the computer. "I'm not super tech-savvy, but that kind of thing can't just happen by accident, can it?"

He hesitates a moment, then shakes his head. "I'm no web designer, but I don't think so." He folds his hands on the desk, copulating gingerbread men forgotten for now. "Can you think of anyone who'd want to mess with you?"

I think back to my high school years. The locker room taunts from cheerleaders as I hunched in a sports bra and used my arms to hide my doughy midsection. The hoots from the lunchroom jocks when I made the mistake of getting in the pizza line instead of the one for salad.

That's all behind me, though, right?

"No," I say. "I haven't had any trouble with anyone."

Not for a long time.

"It seems sort of weird, don't you think?" he asks.

"What seems weird?"

"Well, first you said someone left a gate open last week."

"Sure, but it could have been the wind or something."

Brandon takes a bite of cookie and continues. "You mentioned missing paperwork, when I know for a fact you're the most organized person I've met."

"Sure, but—"

"And you said someone keeps leaving the truck lights on, even though that's not the sort of thing you'd forget," he continues. "Plus, there's this thing with the website."

I frown, wondering if he has a point. Wondering if I should have noticed a pattern sooner. "That seems a little paranoid to put all those things together."

"That seems a little suspicious to have them all happen in a week."

I chew my bottom lip, not liking where this is going. "Maybe," I admit. "I still think it's just a coincidence."

Brandon picks up another gingerbread pair and bites off a leg. At least I think it's a leg. "We had a saying in the Marines," he says. "Let's break it down Barney style."

"Like the purple dinosaur?"

"Bingo." He bites off an arm and chews thoughtfully for a while. "Can you think of anyone who'd want to screw up your stuff?"

I think about Stacey the first-grade teacher and the look she gave me when she thought Brandon and I might be dating. Would she be capable of something like that? Or any of the women who spent the afternoon draping themselves over his lap? Romantic rivalry can be a powerful motivator.

I shake my head, pretty sure that's not the answer. "I don't think so."

"Okay...any interns or new-hires you don't trust?"

I pick at the coconut pubic hair, considering the question. "Just you."

He busts out laughing, sputtering cookie crumbs across my desk. He swipes at them with his arm, shaking his head as he regains his composure. "Can't fault you for your honesty. I guess."

"Sorry. I didn't mean it like that. Just that you're new and—well, different."

"You think I'm here to mess up your farm?"

"No." I shake my head, not sure why I said anything at all. "But I do think you're a distraction."

"From what?"

I sigh and press my fingers to my temples, wondering why I opened this can of worms. "I need to make Jingle Bell Reindeer Ranch a success."

"And you don't think I'm helping with that?"

He's got me there. There's no question that Brandon's presence here has more than doubled the business we'd expected to see. I should be grateful for that. I should be thanking him. I should be down on my knees—

Wait. Where was I going with that?

I clear my throat. "I take this business pretty seriously," I say. "And I do wonder if the novelty of Studmuffin Santa might wear off."

"Fair enough," he says, not looking terribly offended.

"It's nothing personal," I tell him. "I'm just considering the traditionalists. The folks who might not come if they hear Santa is a hot Marine instead of a jolly old grandpa. The success of this place rests on my shoulders, so I need to make smart decisions."

He nods and grabs another cookie. "I thought it was a sister act."

"It is, but I'm the big sister. That means I have a responsibility."

He bites an arm off an alarmingly well-endowed gingerbread man and leans back in his chair. "I get that. I'm an only child, but I've seen that with my cousins. The way they're always looking out for each other. Sometimes when they don't want someone looking out for them at all."

I think about the cousins and their crazy-expensive luxury ranch catering to the highest dollar.

Looking out for themselves, I think but don't say.

"Let me help," he says, and instantly I feel guilty for thinking unkind thoughts about his cousins.

"Help how?"

"I don't like how things are adding up here," he says. "Maybe I'm paranoid, but being super-cautious kept me from getting my face blown off more than once in combat."

I scrape my thumb over a ridge in my desk, not liking the thought of Brandon in danger. "You don't need to get involved."

"I'm already involved," he says. "I'm Santa, remember?"

"How could I forget?"

"Let me keep an extra close eye on things," he insists. "It'll make me feel better knowing someone's watching over you, keeping you safe."

"And you think that someone should be you?"

"You got a better idea?"

I don't. In fact, I can think of no one on earth I'd rather have watching me than Brandon Brown.

And that scares the ever lovin' hell out of me.

"Okay," I say, nodding as I pick up a cookie. "But you have to let me pay you for extra time."

"We can negotiate." He grins and grabs another cookie, making me wonder exactly what sort of bargain I've just made.

CHAPTER 8

BRANDON

Temperatures are mild—both Jade and the weather—for the rest of the week, but it's a relief to have her aware that I'm looking out for her. She may not know Amber started it, but at least I don't have to pretend I'm not double-checking locks and keeping an extra-close watch over the animals.

On Friday, I wake to a thick blanket of snow outside. I sit up in bed, blinking the way I have every morning I've woken up to find myself in a luxury cabin with billion-thread-count sheets and my own private hot tub.

Helping my cousins finish their new resort has its perks.

I slide out of bed and dress quickly, grateful I had the foresight to shower the night before. Reaching the lodge requires shoveling a twenty-foot long path through eight inches of snow, and I'm sweating by the time I get there.

"Morning, cuz."

Sean greets me with a smile and a breakfast burrito, which he hands me before I've had a chance to sit down at one of the live-edge juniper tables that's awaiting a final coat of lacquer.

"Morning," I say, nodding to the wall behind him. "Looks like you've got the bar all set up."

"Just about," he says. "We're still weeks away from the OLCC inspection, but I want to be ready."

Sean slides into the chair across from me as I bite into the warm tortilla stuffed with fluffy egg and roasted peppers and some kind of sausage that tastes like heaven. "So how's the Santa life treating you?" he asks.

"Fine," I mumble through a mouthful of burrito. "My shift starts in a couple hours, but I think I'll head out early and see if they need help moving snow."

My cousin gives me a knowing look and takes a slug of coffee. "You sure the boss ladies don't have anything to do with you wanting to spend more time out there?"

I consider bullshitting him, and maybe I could get away with it. It's not like we were that close as kids, since he and the rest of them grew up in East Coast boarding schools. But any time Uncle Cort came out here to check out his ranch, he'd bring one of the kids. There was a summer my folks were fighting a lot, which meant I spent many nights sharing a bunk bed with Sean. That's probably why he's the one I feel closest to out here.

"Maybe," I admit. "It's dumb, but I keep thinking about her. That smile, the way her hair smells like gingerbread, how she doesn't take any crap from anyone. And those eyes, my God—"

"I hear ya," he says, grinning. "I'm a sucker for brown eyes, too."

"Brown?" I frown at my cousin. "What the hell are you talking about? Jade's eyes are blue."

"Oh." He looks weirdly relieved. "You're hot for Jade?"

"You thought I was talking about the other sister?"

He shrugs and picks up his coffee mug. "Let's just say I've had a thing for Amber since I was a kid."

"I didn't realize you even knew her," I say.

"I don't," he admits, rubbing his palm over a knothole on the edge of the table. "Not really. Which is probably why she's destined to stay my dream girl."

"You're weird."

Sean snorts into his coffee. "Oh, speaking of weird, that Stacey chick stopped by for you again yesterday."

"Stacey Fleming?"

"Yeah. She asked if you were dating anybody." I must look alarmed, because Sean holds up a hand. "Don't worry, I said you'd been seeing someone."

"You did?"

"You said you're not interested, right? In Stacey, I mean. That seemed kinder than telling her to get lost."

"I see your point."

Sean takes a sip of his coffee while I dump more salsa on my breakfast burrito.

"She said something about Jade," Sean says.

"Stacey did?"

He nods. "Yeah. I don't know if she assumed that's who you're dating or—"

"What did she say about Jade?"

Sean looks thoughtful as he takes another sip from his mug. "She made this offhand comment about Jade not being fat anymore. I asked what she meant, and she said Jade was kinda chubby in school. That kids gave her kind of a hard time about it."

"Jade?" That can't be right. "She's like the fiercest woman I know. Who'd be dumb enough to pick on her?"

Sean shrugs. "Could be that's what made her fierce."

Could be. Or maybe Stacey's full of crap. I pick at my breakfast burrito and wonder which it is.

"Anyway, I don't think Jade's interested in me," I tell him. "She's pretty focused on getting her business up and running."

"Not to mention you don't have a reputation for sticking around."

"What do you mean?"

He shrugs and fiddles with a sugar packet in the middle of the table. "I hear things," he says. "From the construction crew guys you went to high school with. You had quite the reputation."

I'm almost afraid to ask. No, I *am* afraid to ask. "I dated a lot of girls in high school," I admit. "But Christ, that was thirteen years ago."

He shrugs. "None of my business. But for some people, it takes a long time to get over all the teenage shit."

"Huh." I don't have anything more clever to say, so I shove the last bite of breakfast burrito in my mouth and wash it down with coffee. "I like to think I've had time to grow up since then."

"I think we all hope for that," he says. He stands up and claps me on the shoulder, then pushes his chair in. "I've gotta run. See you later tonight?"

"Yeah. I'll help you guys install those cabinets in the Larch cabin if you want."

"Sounds good." He turns and walks out of the room, stomping his feet in the snow as the door shuts behind him.

I mull his words as I wash my breakfast dishes and put them away. How much did my high school experiences shape who I turned out to be? Probably a lot, I have to admit. I wonder if the same is true for Jade.

I drive to the reindeer ranch in a mist of snowflakes, careful to keep my speed down and my eyes open for patches of black ice.

I know something's wrong the instant I turn in to the ranch driveway. Maybe it's the fact that there *is* no driveway.

It's covered in a thick layer of snow, untouched by plow or snow-thrower, despite the fact that they open in less than an hour.

A couple hundred feet away, I spot Jade at the top of the drive with a shovel. Her head is down, and her red parka is bright against the glittery snowfield behind her. There's a small mountain of snow to her right, but the length of a football field ahead of her down the driveway.

I ease closer, grateful for the truck's four-wheel-drive. Jade looks up as I approach, her cheeks flushed with exertion.

"Don't tell me you're trying to shovel this whole driveway by hand," I say.

Jade grits her teeth and blows a damp hank of hair off her face. "Our plow truck won't start, and I can't find anyone else who can get out here with a blade before we open," she says.

Alarm rattles through me, and I resist the urge to ask questions. To point out this is one more mysterious thing to go wrong at the ranch. That's not helpful right now.

"Don't you have a snow blower?" I ask.

She shakes her head. "It won't start, either. I have no idea how—"

"I've got it," I tell her. "Go shovel the walks or deal with the reindeer or something, and I'll take care of the driveway."

I flip a U-turn before she has a chance to argue, but I see her standing there with a befuddled expression in my rearview mirror.

It takes me five minutes to get back to my cousins' place, and less than thirty seconds to convince Sean to let me borrow the plow truck. Only fifteen minutes have passed since I left Jade standing here, and already she's made an impressive dent in the walkways.

She looks up when she sees me, and the relief on her face makes me feel like a damn hero.

"Brandon," she says as I finish the first pass and angle the blade to shove a thick slab of snow to the side. "I can't believe you did this. Thank you."

"No problem," I tell her. "You want the next pile over there?"

"At the edge of the parking lot would be perfect," she says. "Amber had this idea about making snowmen or igloos or something with the kids."

"I'll do my best not to dredge up too much gravel."

She shakes her head, her expression somewhere between gratitude and exhaustion. "You're amazing."

I'll admit it, this isn't the first time I've heard someone say that. But it's the first time the words have really socked me in the gut. "You're welcome," I say, and return to plowing.

The snow is thick and soupy, filled with early-season moisture. The driveway takes longer than expected, but we're still doing okay on time when I'm finished with the parking lot. By the time I've parked the rig and gotten out, Jade is standing on the freshly shoveled walkway, conferring with Amber.

"The disability codes say we need to shovel almost twice this wide for all the walkways," Jade is saying. "And we still have to get everyone fed and harnessed for the display."

Amber bites her lip. "We'll never make it in time." She looks up at me and nods. "Maybe Brandon's plow truck could widen the walkways?"

I shake my head and push up the sleeves of my jacket. "It's too big," I tell her. "But if you've got an extra shovel, I can work on that while you take care of the reindeer."

Jade looks miserable. "We can't ask you to do that."

"You didn't ask," I point out. "I'm offering. Now are you going to get me a shovel, or should I take yours?"

She looks like she might want to wrestle me for it, and I can't say I'd mind. "I'll pay you overtime," she says. "I can't possibly thank you enough, but at least I can pay you."

"You can pay me by letting me take you to dinner later. Now where's that extra shovel?"

Jade blinks at me, then turns and walks away. Presumably to get a shovel, though it's anyone's guess. When Jade is out of earshot, Amber leans close and lowers her voice. "Thanks for saving our asses today," she whispers. "She's not very good at taking help from anyone."

"She's getting better at it," I say. "She's even agreed to let me keep an eye on things."

"For real?"

I nod. "She doesn't know that's why you hired me, but—"

"That's not the only reason I hired you." She smiles. "You've been good for business, Brandon. Thank you."

"Don't mention it."

She studies me a moment, something resembling a smirk on her face. "You like her."

"Jade? Sure, she's great. Smart and hard-working and—"

"No, you *like her* like her."

"What is this, fourth grade?"

Amber grins wider as Jade returns with the shovel. She hands it to me with a frown. "Seriously, thank you, Brandon. I don't know what I'd do without you."

"Let's not find out."

Amber turns and heads off toward the reindeer barn, while I set to work shoveling. Jade works from the other end of the building, her movements slow and steady, but effective. It's slow going for both of us, but by nine-fifteen, we have most of the major walkways cleared. I lose sight of her at one point, but I assume she's gone to help Amber deal with the reindeer.

I'm startled to hear her voice behind me. "Here, drink this."

I turn to see Jade holding out a cup in each hand. One looks like water, and the other is a mug of cocoa topped with whipped cream and red and green sprinkles. I lean my shovel up against the barn and reach for both of them. The water goes down in two gulps before I start on the cocoa.

"Thanks."

"No, thank you," she says. "Seriously, Brandon, you saved the day."

"Are the reindeer ready to roll?"

"Yes, and the walkways are clear on both sides of the barn. Thank you."

"No problem." I swig a sip of the cocoa. It's rich and warm and burns all the way down. "I meant what I said about dinner," I tell her.

She rolls her eyes, and my heart curls into a ball at the sight of all that blue in motion. "The point is for *me* to repay *you*," she says. "Not for you to buy me dinner."

"I didn't say I was paying." I wink at her. "Maybe I'll order the lobster."

Her cheeks pinken a little, or maybe it's just the exertion of all that shoveling. "Even that's not enough." She bites her lip, distracting the hell out of me. "I'd offer you a raise, but—"

"You're not technically my boss, remember?"

She frowns. "I still make payroll decisions."

"I don't want your money, Jade."

"What do you want?"

Is it my imagination, or does her voice come out breathy and a little high?

I lean close, so fixated on her mouth that I can't think of anything else. I'm inches from her now, close enough to brush her lips with mine.

So I take a risk and do it. I know it's dumb, but I can't help it. It's the slightest contact, the softest skim of my lips on hers. But there's the promise of more.

That's what I want more than anything.

I draw back and see her pupils dilated, lips still parted and eager.

"Tonight," I tell her.

"Dinner." She nods like she's confirming the appointment, and I smile in agreement.

But dinner's not what I'm hungry for. And I don't know how long I can keep pretending otherwise.

* * *

"Wow. It's still coming down out there." Jade turns away from the window to face me, her brow creased in concern.

I ease myself out of the Santa throne and join her on the other side of the barn. "That's another foot at least," I tell her. "Think we're safe shutting down early?"

"I don't see how we can't," she said. "Not even Studmuffin Santa is enough to make people want to brave roads like this."

A twinge of frustration pinches at my chest. If no one's getting in, no one's getting out, either, which means the odds of us making it into town for dinner tonight are slim.

Disappointment must register on my face, because she offers a halfhearted smile. "We can do dinner some other time," she says. "Or I could probably throw something together here. It won't be lobster, but—"

"Sold," I say, willing to eat out of the garbage disposal if it means even another hour with Jade.

She smiles and tosses her ponytail over one shoulder. "I'm not the best cook, but I make a decent shrimp scampi. There's even a guest room if you can't make it out tonight."

"Thanks." I wonder if she's forgotten about the plow blade on the front of my truck, and the fact that I could probably make it back to the ranch if another eight feet fell. If Jade invites me to stay, I'm staying.

"Hey, guys." Amber marches in, stomping snow from her boots. "Have you seen Zak?"

"He went to put the camera gear in his truck," Jade says. "Though I'm not sure he'll be able to drive home."

"I pulled down the snowshoes from the attic," she says. "We're heading over to his mom's place for her birthday dinner. It's just a couple miles away, and it'll be fun."

Jade frowns. "I don't want you snowshoeing home alone in the dark. This is cougar country, Amber."

"His brother can bring me home in their plow truck," she assures us. "Or I'll stay in his mom's guest room. Don't worry."

"I can go get you, too," I offer. "If you're really in a jam."

Amber smiles. "See?" she says to Jade. "All taken care of. And I've got all the reindeer fed and bunked down for the night. You okay to finish tidying up in here?"

"No problem," Jade says. "Go on, have fun."

She swats her younger sister on the butt, earning a squeal from Amber as she hustles out the door with two pairs of snowshoes in hand.

"I'll go change out of the Santa suit," I tell Jade. "Then I can help with the rest of the cleanup."

"There's not much to do," she says. "It was so slow today that I got almost everything done already."

"In that case, I'll be quick."

I head into the bathroom to get rid of the Santa costume, folding it carefully into my gym bag while Jade clatters around in the barn. I step out of the restroom to find Jade waiting for me.

"Ready?"

"Yes," she says, and leads me out the door.

Our breath is thick and foggy as we pick our way across the snow-covered path from the barn to the house.

"Is Amber safe out there?"

"Yeah, she's crazy-athletic," Jade says. "Always was. Went to college on a soccer scholarship."

"I wasn't worried about her fitness as much as cougars."

Jade shrugs. "She's got bear spray and a .357 snub nose for protection. You have to out here."

"Jeez. You two really are pioneer women."

Jade grins and sweeps her flashlight beam over the glittery field of snow. "That's the idea."

I kick through a snowdrift and study the house as we approach. It has a wide wraparound porch and old-fashioned lamp posts glowing on either side of the walkway. "So is Amber back with her ex?" I ask.

"Nah," she says, reaching out to knock a thick column of snow off a fencepost. "But she's stayed close with his family. His mom's been like a surrogate mother to her since ours left for Hawaii."

"Is she dating that PI guy instead?"

Jade turns and looks at me, her honey hair glowing with moonlight as she tilts her head to one side. "I don't know. My sister has lots of men fawning over her. Why, you want to ask her out?"

"Your sister?" I shake my head and consider telling her about Sean. That's the real reason for my interest.

But that's not my secret to share, and besides, I know how Jade feels about the resort people. She probably wouldn't want one dating her sister.

"Not my type," I tell her honestly.

"What is your type?"

She looks at me as she reaches out to unlock the door, and I hold her gaze and smile. "The type who makes out with me in barns and pickups and then feeds me scampi."

Her cheeks go bright pink, and she turns away to pull open the front door. "God, you're such a flirt."

It's true, maybe. I suppose I have that reputation. But I'm not just flirting with Jade. This isn't a game to me, like some teenage dalliance. I'm not sure how to get that across to her.

I step into the foyer and look around to see a set of stairs leading up and one headed down. I've always loved split level homes, and this one feels extra cozy with a bank of family photos on one wall and an overflowing wrought iron coat rack parked beside an antique oak bench.

Jade sits down to pry off her boots, and I do likewise, conscious of her hip bumping mine. "Is this the house you grew up in?"

"Yeah. There's a pillar downstairs where our mom used to mark our height every year on the first day of school. We can't bear to paint over it."

"Do you see your folks very often?"

She sets her boots aside and massages her foot, which is clad in a pink and orange polka-dotted sock. It's more whimsical than I would have expected, and I find myself absurdly wondering what sort of panties she wears.

"Our folks were here in June to see some of the newborn calves," she says. "And Amber and I got to visit them in Hawaii last November."

"Do you miss them?"

She nods and lifts her other foot to massage the ball of it. "Yes, but living here helps. Being in the house where they raised us. It's a little dated, but we've been pouring all our money into reindeer stuff. Fixing up barns and paying for feed, not to mention the weddings."

"Weddings?" I don't know why the word startles me so much. "Who's getting married?"

She laughs, which makes me wonder if I sounded a little too alarmed. "Lots of people," she says. "I hope, anyway. That's what we're trying to do in the off-season. Old fashioned country weddings."

"That sounds cool," I say. "I know my cousins are planning something like that at Ponderosa Ranch."

The second I utter the words, I can tell it's the wrong thing to say. Jade's expression darkens, and she starts up the stairs in sock feet. "Come on. Let's get you fed."

I stand up and follow Jade up the battered hardwood staircase and into a brightly lit kitchen. Copper pots dangle from a rack that hangs over a cement-block island. I run my hand over the smooth surface while she starts pulling things out of the fridge.

"I love this," I say. "I've never seen a concrete counter."

"Thanks. Amber and I did it ourselves after watching a couple YouTube videos."

I stare at her, not even bothering to hide my amazement. I sit down on one of her barstools and watch as she lines up ingredients on the counter. "Can I ask you something?"

"Sure." She plunks a bag of frozen shrimp on the counter and starts unwrapping a stick of butter.

"Is there anything you're not insanely good at?"

She looks up with a wary expression. "What do you mean?"

"Well, you're smart—I mean, you're running your own business and you went to veterinary school. You're obviously good at home improvement stuff, plus you can cook—"

"Not well."

"I burn tap water, so it's relative." I spot a bowl of almonds on the counter and grab a handful, hoping they're not reindeer food or something.

"I roasted those with rosemary and olive oil," Jade says. "I saw it in a Martha Stewart thing online, and it looked pretty easy."

"See?" I pop a few almonds in my mouth and chew. "You said you're not much of a cook, but you've obviously got mad kitchen skills. Plus, you're funny, you're kind, you're beautiful. It's like you have everything going for you, so I figure you must have a fault of some kind."

"Buddy, you have no idea." She shakes her head and stretches up to grab a copper colander from the rack overhead. I should probably offer to help, but I'm enjoying the swath of bare stomach as her sweater hikes up. Her skin is creamy and soft-looking, and I'm struck by the urge to bury my face in her belly button.

Jade lowers herself back down to her heels and dumps some frozen shrimp in the colander before running it under the tap to thaw them. I grab another couple almonds.

"I can't pronounce the word 'specifically,'" she says, hair framing her face as she looks down into the sink. "Not without sounding it out really, really slowly."

"What?"

"You asked what I'm not good at, and that's one thing," she says. "If I just say it without thinking, it comes out sounding like 'su-spiff-a-klee.'"

I laugh and watch her fill a big dutch oven with water. She tosses in a pinch of salt and cranks the heat beneath it before turning to grab a box of angel hair pasta from the cupboard.

"What can I do to help?" I ask, nodding to the head of romaine sitting on the counter. "I'm a lousy cook, but I can toss a mean salad."

"Go for it," she says. "And thanks."

I get to my feet and move around to the other side of the counter, grateful for the excuse to stand next to her. Jade's hip bumps my thigh as she moves past me to grab a pair of oven mitts from the drawer beside me, and I resist the urge to lean into her.

"So is that your one thing?" she asks. "The fact that you can't cook, that's what you're bad at?"

"Oh, there are tons of things I'm bad at," I tell her as I slice into a thick tomato, spattering juice all over the cutting board. "I have the opposite of a green thumb. The red thumb of death? Whatever it is when you kill plants just by looking at them."

She laughs and starts throwing things into a saucepan. Butter and garlic and Dijon mustard and a few other things I had no idea went into scampi. She gives it a stir, then turns and reaches for a loaf of French bread.

"I can't imagine you've had much demand for nurturing houseplants in the Marines," she says. "So that's probably not a fatal flaw."

I shrug and begin slicing carrots, sending a tumble of little orange coins over the edge of the cutting board. "So what else are you bad at?" I ask. "Tell me some more things the Mighty Jade can't do perfectly."

"Mighty Jade?" she snorts. "Okay, Wonder Boy. Let me think."

Steam rises from the pot of boiling water, and the whole kitchen is getting warm. Jade strips off her flannel overshirt, leaving her in a snug-fitting red thermal top with little buttons on the front. On most girls, it would look bland, but on Jade, it looks stunning. I ache to undo those buttons one by one. Maybe with my teeth.

"I can't exercise," she says. "I hate the gym and running and weightlifting, which probably explains a lot about my formative years." She gives me a sidelong glance like she's waiting for me to say something, and I remember what Stacey told Sean. I'm not dumb enough to bring that up, though, so I just nod.

"Whatever you're doing seems to work," I tell her. "Not that you need any validation from me, but you've got a rockin' bod."

She snorts. "Farm labor will do that."

I nod and scrape up chopped carrot with the side of my hand so I can toss it into the big blue bowl she just handed me. "I guess I'm the opposite," I tell her. "I can't *not* exercise. It's not that I need to work out all the time to be all buff and macho. I do it because I'm kind of a basket case if I don't. Handling anxiety—there's another thing I'm bad at."

She smiles and checks the temperature on the stove, fiddling with one of the dials. "Let's see," she says. "There's plenty of other stuff I suck at. I can't get through *Pride and Prejudice*. Or most Jane Austen novels, really. I try and try, but I fall asleep before I even get to any good kissy stuff."

The word "kiss" coming from Jade's perfect lips makes me want to shove aside this salad bowl and press her up against the counter. But I focus on chopping romaine instead, determined to keep my hands busy while my brain fishes for something else to share. Some other intimate detail to prolong this conversation so she'll keep offering me delicious little details about herself.

"I'm completely tone deaf," I tell her. "But I really love music, and I love singing along. Or trying to sing along."

"Do you ever sing in front of people?"

"Nope. Only in the shower."

"I'd love to see that."

Her expression goes from amusement to dismay as she realizes what she just said. Then she gets a funny look on her face, and I know she's picturing it. I'm picturing it, too, imagining Jade standing naked under the spray, her breasts smooth and soapy as I help lather shampoo in her hair.

The thought of singing while I do it kinda puts a damper on the fantasy, but still.

"I can't eat candy canes," I blurt, desperate to tamp down the boner that's threatening to embarrass me in the middle of the damn kitchen. "Or any peppermint candy."

"Are you allergic?"

"Nah, it's nothing like that." I look down at the cutting board, a little mortified to be telling this story. "When I was eight, I sucked a candy cane into this pointy little spear."

"Amber and I used to do that." She smiles. "Then we'd have swordfights until our mom made us stop."

"Yeah, my mom told me to knock it off, too," I tell her. "But I didn't listen. And I ended up stabbing a big hole in my tongue."

"Oh, God." Jade stops smiling.

"Took five stitches to close it up, and I wasn't able to eat much for Christmas dinner." I shrug and whack the end off the romaine with my knife. "But my mom made me pumpkin-flavored ice cream instead, which is kind of an awesome substitute when you're eight."

"Ouch." Jade shakes her head. "What happened to your mom?" she asks after a long pause. "If you don't mind me asking. You mentioned she left, but you never said where she went."

"Honestly, I have no idea," I tell her. "My Uncle Cort tracked her down to Florida about ten years ago so she could sign some paperwork. But now I don't know whether she's alive or dead."

"She's never tried to contact you?"

I shake my head. "Nope. Not once."

"God. I'm so sorry."

I'm more sorry, both for dragging down our conversation, and for dragging Jade into this. Then again, I want her to know. I want her to understand there's more to me than Studmuffin

Santa or Wonder Boy or Hometown Hero or whatever else she thinks of when she sees me.

Why does it matter so much that she knows it?

"It's fine now," I tell her. "My tongue is perfectly functional."

"I noticed."

I look up from the cutting board to see her flushing bright pink.

"Speaking," she adds. "I meant your tongue works for speaking."

I grin and return to my task. "I'm not always great at that, either," I tell her. "Saying what I want to say. But I manage."

She dumps the colander of shrimp into the bubbling sauce and stirs, her shoulder bumping mine as she moves to slide the pasta into the water. "I guess it's understandable you'd have a bit of Christmas baggage."

I see an opening and take it, seizing the chance to change the subject. "Want to hear a dirty joke that one of the older kids told me yesterday?"

"I'm not sure, do I?"

"Yep." I grin. "Speaking of Christmas baggage."

"Okay, go."

"Know why Santa's sack is so big?"

Jade looks leery, glancing at me like she's not sure she wants to hear the punchline. "Why is Santa's sack so big?"

"Because he only comes once a year."

She gives an exaggerated groan, but she's smiling, so I know I haven't offended her. I'm glad I've managed to move the conversation back to lighthearted turf. To steer us away from the ghosts of Christmas past and back into this cozy kitchen that's filled with the scent of warm pasta water and the lilt of music.

It takes me a moment to recognize it's Christmas music, and I wonder when she switched it on. I also wonder when I started humming along with it.

"You have a nice voice," she says as she soaps up the colander, then rinses it. "Maybe you can't sing, but you can hum."

"Remind me to add that to my Santa résumé."

She smiles and sets the colander back in the sink, then uses a pair of tongs to flip the shrimp. "I can't flirt."

Her confession is quieter than the others, and it takes me a second to process what she's said. "Flirt?"

"Right, with guys. I end up putting my foot in my mouth and saying ridiculous things."

She switches off both burners and pulls on a pair of oven mitts before carrying the pot of water to the sink. She dumps out the pasta into the colander, not meeting my eyes as she shakes out the water.

"Flirting's overrated," I tell her.

"Spoken by a guy who's a pro," she says.

I can't argue with that, so I don't try. Then again, I feel like all my normal skills with women fly right out the window when it comes to Jade. I concentrate on dumping the rest of my salad fixings into the big blue bowl while Jade shovels the pasta into the pot with the sauce and shrimp. She gives it a stir, looking thoughtful and a little bit sheepish.

"Okay, I just thought of one more thing I'm bad at," she says.

"What's that?"

"I can't roll my tongue." She sticks it out in illustration, and it takes me a second to figure out what she's talking about.

"See?" she says, though it comes out more like *"thee"* since she's got her tongue sticking out. It's flat as a paperback, no curve at all, and I can't decide if it's adorable or hot as hell. Maybe both.

"Oh, you mean curling it? Like this?" I stick out my own tongue, easily curving the edges so it rolls like a cigar.

Jade busts out laughing. "Yes, that's it! Exactly! It's a genetic thing, I guess. Amber can't do it either."

She tries again, making a silly face. Those blue eyes dance with merriment, and all I can think about is her mouth. Her lips, her tongue, how much I want to taste her again. It's the most ridiculous thing in the world as we stand here making silly faces at each other, but I'm aching with the urge to kiss her.

So I do.

I take a step forward, and she pulls her tongue back into her mouth. She looks at me with those lake-blue eyes as I slide my hands around her waist. I pause there, giving her a chance to pull back if she doesn't want this. It's hardly the world's smoothest seduction, and I can't blame her if she's not turned on by chopping veggies and telling dirty jokes and playing silly tongue curling games.

But she doesn't pull back. She moves willingly against me, lips parting as I draw her close and brush my mouth over hers.

"Brandon," she whispers, and the sound of my name in that soft, gentle voice makes something uncoil inside me.

I slide my fingers into her hair, wondering when she took it down. Why I can't seem to get enough of her. I kiss her then, and she kisses back, hands coming up to twine around my neck.

She gives a soft little moan and deepens the kiss, urging me on. I slide my hands down, cupping her perfect backside as I press her up against the counter and hope like hell she turned off the burner. It would be just my luck we'd catch her hair on fire.

But, no, she's moving against me now, making those soft little noises in the back of her throat that drive me crazy. I pry my hands off her ass and glide up, taking my time tracing her ribs beneath her thermal shirt. She presses into me as my palms skim the undersides of her breasts.

Jade breaks the kiss and looks up at me, her blue eyes wild and her breath coming fast. "How hungry are you?"

"For dinner?"

She nods and licks her lips.

"Not very," I admit.

"Then hang on." She pulls away and grabs a lid off the counter, plunking it onto the pot with a clang. She picks up the whole thing with a pair of oven mitts and shoves it into the fridge. Then she turns and tosses aside the mitts.

"Will you come upstairs with me?"

I nod, hoping like hell I understand the invitation. That she's not just asking me up there to play Monopoly or read comic books. Even if that were true, I'd go willingly. I'd follow her off the end of a pier.

"Yes," I say, and it comes out sounding weirdly breathless. "I'd love that."

"Come on." She grabs me by the hand and turns to pull me down a narrow hallway.

CHAPTER 9

JADE

I've thought about this since I was fourteen years old.

Well, not *this,* exactly. I was pretty naïve about sex at fourteen, but I knew enough to understand why I felt tingly when Brandon Brown trotted out onto that football field in his tight pants.

As I shove my bedroom door shut behind us and turn to face him, I can't help thinking he looks damn fine in jeans, too.

"What's got you smiling?" he murmurs as he takes a step closer. His thumb grazes the underside of my chin, tilting my face up so he can kiss me again.

God, I could never get tired of kissing this guy.

I'm breathless again by the time we break apart, and I've almost forgotten what he asked. "This," I whisper. "I've thought about this for a long time."

He smiles and kisses me again, edging me back toward the bed as he tunnels his fingers in my hair. I grab for the hem of his shirt and tug, desperate to have it off him. To rake my fingers up those bare abs and to feel that soft, springy hair pressed against me.

Brandon breaks the kiss and helps me with the shirt, tossing it aside before meeting my eyes again. "You sure about this?" he asks.

I nod and reach for the hem of my own shirt. I try for one of those sexy crossed-arm maneuvers, but my thermal undershirt is snug and my hair gets tangled in the armpit and I'm dizzy by the time I find myself standing topless in front of him.

He smiles and reaches out to skim a palm over the lace edge of my bra. "You're beautiful." He draws his thumb over my ribcage, leaning down to peer at the tattoo there. "Is that a heart in a magnifying glass?"

I nod, my emotions somewhere between self-consciousness and dizzying desire. "Yes," I murmur. "It's from *How the Grinch Stole Christmas*. The part where his heart grew three sizes?"

He laughs and leans down to plant a kiss on the spot. "I'd totally forgotten that book."

"I got the ink a couple years ago when Amber and I started talking about this crazy reindeer thing," I say. "It's a reminder of why we started it. What it's all about for us."

"I love it," he says, and I'm not sure if he's talking about the tattoo or the story behind it. He kisses me again, and I shiver as every nerve in my core sizzles to attention.

I reach out to touch his chest, his abs, his arms. I can't get enough of him, and he feels even better than I imagined. He lays me down on the bed, and I go willingly, eager to feel his weight on top of me.

We take our time kissing, making out like teenagers rounding the bases from first to second to third—

"God, Jade," he gasps as he circles his tongue over my nipple. My bra is long gone and so are my pants, though I'm still wearing panties. I wriggle against him, wondering whether I unzipped his jeans or he did. I slide a hand inside them, making us both gasp.

"You're driving me crazy," he murmurs against my breast.

"Don't stop."

"I want you so much."

I arch against him, urging him to keep going. To take this to the next level. I stroke him through his underwear, not the least bit surprised by his impressive length. Of course Wonder Boy would be hung like a horse.

He brushes his lips across mine before angling back to look at me. "Um, do you happen to have any, uh—"

"Venereal diseases?"

He looks alarmed, so I shake my head. "No! Definitely not."

He smiles and plants a kiss along my hairline. "I was going to say 'condoms,' but thanks for clarifying."

I grimace and blow a few strands of hair off my forehead. "No," I admit, feeling deflated. "I wasn't exactly planning to cap off my snow day by banging Santa."

He laughs and slides down my body so he's kneeling at the edge of the bed. "So we have a problem, then," he says, planting a kiss on my hipbone. "In my haste to get here with the plow truck, I left my wallet at home."

Disappointment surges through me. Silly me, I assumed a guy like Brandon Brown would have condoms on him at all times. "I guess I should be relieved you don't stash prophylactics in your Santa suit."

He laughs and plants a kiss on my belly. "That would be a shock for all those moms who've been fishing in my pockets for candy canes."

There's a flare of jealousy in my stomach, but it dissipates the instant I feel Brandon's warm breath against my belly button. He kisses me there, and I squirm with equal parts pleasure and ticklishness.

"So I suppose we should stop," I murmur, not wanting to at all.

He shakes his head, eyes glittering with desire. "No way," he says, hooking his thumbs in the edges of my panties. Instinct has me lifting my hips so he can draw them down, sliding them slowly over my legs and onto the floor. I start to press my legs together, self-conscious to be the only naked one in the room.

But he shoulders my thighs apart. "I'm dying to taste you," he says.

Oh, God.

His hands are on my hips, and my whole body is throbbing like the drumbeat in an up-tempo Christmas tune. "Brandon," I gasp, and slide my fingers into his hair.

He plants a kiss on my hipbone, then another on my thigh. A million little kisses landing in unexpected spots until I'm breathless and squirming and dizzy with need. I arch up, torn between feeling bad about the condoms and desperate for more. For anything he can offer.

At last, he gives me what I'm aching for. Just the lightest little flick of his tongue, but I cry out like it's the first time anyone's touched me.

"Jesus," I gasp, clawing at his hair.

"You're so wet."

I moan as his tongue glides along my center, dipping, circling, teasing. He grips my hips with both hands, angling me up to meet his mouth. I let go of his hair and grab fistfuls of my comforter, tipping my head back to savor the sensation.

His mouth is magical, soft and gentle and so very aware of every spot that feels fucking amazing. It's like there's a homing device in the tip of his tongue.

"So sweet," he murmurs against me. "You're so sweet."

I cry out as sensation starts to build inside me. It's slow at first, but then comes swirling at me like a tornado. He slides two fingers into me, and that's all it takes. I scream as the first wave takes me, clutching the duvet like it's the only thing anchoring me to the bed. His fingers move inside me, tongue circling and stroking and driving me mindless. I cry out again, grateful my sister's not home and that Brandon knows how to keep teasing, how to coax every last pulse of pleasure from my body.

When I finally come down, he slides up my thighs and moves beside me on the bed. He pulls me so I'm curled against him, and I reach for his fly, conscious of the fact that he's probably dying for his own release.

But he makes a shushing sound in my hair and plants a kiss along my ear. "There'll be other times for that," he says. "Just lie back and relax."

And for the first time in forever, I do.

* * *

I WAKE the next morning to a glass of water and a note on my nightstand. I roll over into a sunbeam, feeling decadent and warm and thoroughly sated.

JADE,

Last night was amazing. YOU are amazing.

I heard Amber come home at midnight and I didn't want things to be awkward for you, so I slipped out when she was in her room. Hope that's okay. I can't wait to see you tomorrow.

P.S. The scampi was delicious. I left plenty for you.

I FOLD the note into my nightstand, conscious of the fact that I'm grinning like a big, fat idiot.

I pull on a robe and pad barefoot down the hall to my sister's room. I lift my hand to knock, but she calls out before I have a chance.

"Come on in," she says. "I'm already up."

Pushing the door open, I spot her sitting at the dressing table we've had since we were little girls. Our mom used to sit us down one at a time to comb our hair, her fingers gently working out wild tangles.

She smiles at me in the mirror, her expression the tiniest bit smug. "Look at you all lovey-faced. It's like the reindeer when they're in heat."

I pick up her hairbrush and give her a light whack on the head. Then I set to work brushing her hair, something I haven't done for years.

"Mmm," she murmurs as I run the brush through my sister's dark waves. "That feels nice."

"You stole my conditioner again," I reply, not really minding.

"It smells like gingerbread," she says. "I kinda want to eat it."

"Please don't," I mutter. "Remember what happened to Prancer when he tried to eat the soap?"

"Ugh," she says with a giggle. "He blew butt bubbles for three days."

I keep brushing, the dark strands sleek and shiny as the bristles glide through her hair. "How was dinner with Zak's family?"

"Fine. His brother brought me home around midnight." Her eyes meet mine in the mirror, and she gives an inquisitive eyebrow lift. "So Brandon was here late."

I consider not responding. Or telling a small fib about him staying late to shovel snow or help with paperwork. But the flush in my cheeks gives me away.

"Yeah," I admit. "I offered to make him dinner."

Her grin gets bigger. "From the looks of you, that's not all you offered him."

"We didn't sleep together," I blurt, which just sounds silly.

Amber laughs. "I'm not prying," she says. "I'm not judging, either. Frankly, I'd be glad if you did sleep with him."

"Why?"

"Why?" She rolls her eyes. "Because it wouldn't hurt you to date a little bit. Especially someone as hot as Brandon Brown."

I shake my head and drag the brush down the back of her head, earning a sound like a purr. "I don't have room in my life for dating," I say. "And even if I did, can you really picture me with someone like him?"

"You mean a hot, sexy war hero who's good with kids and generous with his plowing?" Amber gives a suggestive eyebrow wiggle on *plowing*, then puts a finger to her chin and pretends to consider it. "Gee, let me think . . . uh, *hell, yes*!"

I laugh at her theatrics, even though I'm not sure I believe the sentiment behind it. "He's a bit out of my league," I point out. "The quarterback and the farm girl? It sounds like a bad romance novel."

Amber rolls her eyes. "You're not a girl and he's not a quarterback. For God's sake, Jade, you're a grown-ass woman and he's a grown-ass man. I would hope you've both moved past whoever the hell you were as kids."

I stroke the brush through her hair again and wonder if she has a point. I'm certainly different than the person I was at sixteen. Maybe I'm not giving Brandon enough credit for moving beyond his teenage self.

"Speaking of high school," Amber says, and there's an odd note in her voice that snaps my attention back to her face. I watch her in the mirror, aware that she's choosing her words carefully. "Zak's mom gave me a box of photos last night."

"Of what?"

"Stuff he took in high school. Did you know he was on the yearbook staff?"

"Maybe," I say. "He was a couple grades below me, so we didn't really know each other."

"Yeah, but I guess the middle school yearbook kids got to shoot a lot of high school stuff. Candid things around the school and at sports events and stuff."

Something's different in her expression, and I force myself to hold her gaze in the mirror. I wonder what's making her look at me with this odd mix of sadness and curiosity. "Was there something that caught your eye?" I ask.

She nods, and I could swear her eyes glitter just a bit. "Yeah. A couple shots of you hunched over on a bench in the lunchroom, sitting all alone." She hesitates. "You looked miserable. I didn't realize—I guess I never—"

She stops, and I'm not positive what she's trying to say. But I have an idea.

"You were a lot younger than me," I murmur. "I was glad things were better for you by the time you got to high school. The sports stuff helped."

"But you—didn't have a good experience?"

I shrug and glance away, focusing my attention on a snarl at the nape of her neck. "It wasn't great."

"So it's true then," she says softly. "Were you bullied?"

I hold my breath, considering how much to tell her. How much I want her to know. "It wasn't that bad."

She must hear something in my voice. I'm never a very good liar. "Yes, it was," she says. "It was exactly that bad."

"Yeah," I admit, forcing the word out through a throat that's getting tighter by the second. "It was."

I clear my throat, wondering if I should stop talking. If I should spare her false memories of me as the cheerful, well-adjusted big sister. The one with plump cheeks and a dimpled smile for family instead of the one cowering in corners of the lunchroom.

There's no reason she needs to know the whole story, right?

I meet her eyes in the mirror and realize she does want to know. She deserves to.

I take a shaky breath and begin.

"I remember in art class, freshman year, I made this clay pig," I say. "Mom and dad had just bought all those Red Wattles, and I thought they were so cool."

Amber's eyes hold mine in the mirror, and she nods once, urging me on. I draw the brush down slowly, still keeping up the pretense of the task. "Anyway, a bunch of sophomore jocks cornered me in the hall after class," I say. "They started calling me Miss Piggy, making oinking noises, that sort of thing."

"Jesus."

"I wasn't a skinny kid," I say. "So the teasing stung. Anyway, one of them grabbed the pig from me. Matthew Lerten or Brian Grimes or one of those guys. They started tossing it around, playing keep away. I was running back and forth, crying and begging them to give it back."

"Oh, Jade."

My throat gets tight again, and it takes a few more breaths before I can force the rest of the words out. "Brandon came walking down the hall then. He didn't know who I was, but a couple of the guys had made varsity that year, so I guess he knew them from football."

"Did he say something to you?"

My hands stop moving and the brush stills in her hair. "No," I say. "Not to me. He didn't say a word to me."

"Oh." She waits in breathless silence, knowing there's more.

"But he did say something to the guys," I continue. "He grabbed the pig out of the air and handed it to me without looking." I swallow hard, determined to force out the rest of the words. Determined not to cry. "Then he told the guys to knock it the fuck off. Walked away without another word."

"Oh my God." A tear slips down Amber's cheek, and it kills me to see her so broken up over something that happened such a long time ago. Something I'm positive Brandon doesn't remember.

"I'm sure it wasn't even a blip on his radar," I tell her. "But it meant a lot to me." I give a hollow little laugh. "I guess it must have been November then, because Christmas cards were out on the shelf at Freddies. I bought one and stuck it in his locker."

"What did it say?"

I shrug, not positive I remember exactly. "Something about

him being a nice guy," I say. "I didn't sign my name or anything. He wouldn't have known it anyway."

"Wow," she says. "So is that why you didn't want me to hire him?"

"It wasn't that, exactly," I say. "I just didn't think I wanted that reminder in my life. Something I've worked hard to put behind me."

She nods and swipes the back of her hand under her eye. "You could have told me, you know."

I shake my head and run the brush through her hair again. There are no tangles left, but it feels nice to glide the bristles through those glossy strands. "I didn't want to relive all that."

"Still," she says. She must sense I want to change the subject. That I'm ready to move on. "So how are things now?" she asks. "With Brandon, I mean."

I can't help it. My face breaks into a stupid grin, and I find myself blushing. "Good," I admit. "Really good."

"I'm glad," she says. "You deserve it." She stands up and turns to face me, and for a second, I think we're going to hug.

Instead, she grabs the brush from my hand. "You know what else you deserve?"

"What?"

"Someone brushing your hair for a change."

"I don't need—"

"Sit!" she commands, and I do.

I ease into the chair, sighing with pleasure as Amber pulls the brush along my scalp. It feels heavenly, soft and soothing, like scratching an itch I didn't know was there.

"See?" she says. "It feels good to have someone take care of you sometimes."

I meet her eyes in the mirror and nod. "Yeah," I murmur. "It kinda does."

* * *

"There you go," I say, handing a pair of photos to a young mother in a startlingly low-cut Christmas sweater. "Here's the one of the boys next to Blitzen, and the other one of all three of you with Santa."

"Mmm, this one's yummy, don't you think?"

I'm honestly not sure if she means Santa, Zak's photography skills, or the candy cane she just nabbed from the bowl beside the Christmas tree, but I nod anyway and pretend not to notice the hungry look she shoots at Brandon's backside as he stands up from the Santa throne and bends down to collect his things.

"You'll be here for two more weeks?" she asks. "All the way up to Christmas day?"

"Not Mondays," I tell her. "But every day besides that. And after that, we shift into wedding season. There's information about it on our website if you know anyone who's getting married."

"Mmm," she says again, still eyeing Brandon. "Maybe if I find the right guy. It gets so lonely being a single mom, you know?"

She says these last words to Brandon, who has stepped up beside me and put a hand on my shoulder. The mom frowns and turns on her heel, seeming to remember that she has offspring she should locate.

"They're washing up in the bathroom," Amber says as she walks up and joins us. "We were over there at the craft table painting pictures of the reindeer."

"Of course," says Single Mom Barbie, smiling once more at Brandon before turning to collect her kids. "I'll see you around," she says. "I'm coming back next week with eight women from my Mommy-and-Me yoga class."

"I look forward to visiting with the kids," says Brandon politely as she sashays out the front door. Amber hurries to lock it behind them.

Brandon turns to me and offers a sexy smile. "Hey there."

"Hey yourself."

He grins and leans against the Santa throne. "We haven't had two seconds to say hello all day. How are you doing?"

"I'm good," I say, fighting hard to keep a goofy smile from creeping over my face. "Thanks for the note."

"Thanks for last night," he murmurs, leaning close. "I was thinking maybe later we could—"

"Hey, Bran!"

I jump back from Brandon and turn to see Stacey Fleming standing in the doorway at the opposite end of the barn, gripping the hand of a reluctant-looking toddler.

"I know you guys are closed," she says, "but my niece is in town for just the day, and I promised her Santa is a good friend of mine who wouldn't mind spending just a few minutes with us."

I see Brandon's jaw working as he grits his teeth, but he manages a friendly Santa smile. "Sure," he says, adjusting his faux facial hair. "Come on over."

Stacey struts across the room, leading the cherubic toddler by the hand.

"Our photographer went home already," I tell her. "And my sister just took the last reindeer back to the barn."

Stacey waves a hand like that's irrelevant. "We're just here for Santa."

Brandon gives me a pained look as he settles back in his chair. Stacey clambers onto his lap and pulls the adorable niece up, too, and I have to look away from all that cute in one place.

There's a knock at the door on the other side of the barn, so I leave this happy little scene and go to answer it. Throwing open the heavy wood panel, I'm greeted by a sweet-faced brunette with Betty Boop curls and Bettie Page curves.

"Can I help you?" I ask.

"I'm Bree. From Ponderosa Luxury Ranch Resort." She nods toward Brandon and lowers her voice. "Also Santa's cousin, though I'd better skip greeting him so he doesn't break character."

I'm torn between feeling annoyed she's here or grateful for the consideration. Either way, I can't very well leave her standing out in the cold.

"Come on in," I tell her. "You're here for your meeting with Amber?"

She nods and steps in, and I can't help admiring her pixie-like features. She's tiny, but something about her seems fierce. "Yes, but I'm early. Sorry, I didn't realize how close our ranches are to each other. I can wait in my car if you want."

"No, it's fine. Come on, you can hang out in the office where it's warm."

I lead her across the barn, smiling a little as she gives Brandon a covert wave before continuing through to the office. I offer her a seat, then stand there debating about whether to leave her alone or wait with her for Amber.

She saves me the trouble of making a decision. "Actually, I was wondering if I could talk to you a second."

"Me? I mostly handle the animals. Amber's the business and marketing side of the—"

"It's not about business," she says, then nods at the door. "May I?"

I assume she's asking to close it and not to exit, so I nod. "Sure."

I wait while she pushes the door shut and reseats herself with hands on her lap. "So I understand you've got something going on with my cousin."

"What?" I choke out. "Did he say that?"

"Not to me, to my brother." She shrugs. "But I'm a nosy little sister, so—"

"Yeah, I know how that goes," I mutter. "I have one of my own."

Bree glances toward the door again, then lowers her voice. "Has he talked to you about his parents?"

I nod, surprised we're going down this path mere seconds

into our first meeting. "Yes." I rest my hands on the desk, determined to be cautious with how much I reveal. "I understand why Christmas isn't his favorite time of year."

"It's not just that. Brandon's terrified of relationships. He watched his dad go from being a happy husband and father to—to—well, practically a vegetable. That'll mess with a guy."

"I see," I say slowly. "It must have been hard."

"He blames his mom for a lot of it," she says. "Actually, that's not true. He blames marriage. Or love, maybe. Anyway, you have to understand why Brandon swore off all of that years ago."

I nod, not sure what she's trying to tell me. To stay away from Brandon? I stay silent, hoping she'll clue me in.

"Be careful." Bree sighs. "He might look big and tough, but he's soft and squishy on the inside. And so very, very sweet."

"I know," I reply, surprised to realize it's true. I've seen Brandon's soft side, probably more than she knows. "Look, if it's any comfort to you, we're not really that serious. I don't think."

"No?"

I shrug. "We hardly know each other."

"Well, I know Brandon. And I can tell by looking at him that he's in deep. And if you hurt him, so help me God, I'll—"

"Hey, sorry I'm late." My sister rushes through the door breathless and tousled. "I'm Amber," she says, holding out her hand. "You must be Bree Bracelyn?"

Bree stands and returns the handshake. "You're not late at all. It's a pleasure to meet you, Amber."

I sit there staring for a moment, still trying to figure out if Bree just threatened me. What was she starting to say?

Bree swings her gaze back to mine and holds for just a moment. There's a warning there, a clear one. She blinks and it's gone, replaced by a friendly, businesslike smile. "Jade and I were just getting to know each other," Bree says. "I can't believe we've been neighbors all this time and we've never met."

"I suppose we've all been busy getting new businesses off the ground," I offer. I stand up, ready to leave Amber to her meeting. "I should get out of your hair—"

"Actually, it would be great if you stayed," Amber says, shooting me a look. "It might be easiest to have this conversation with all three of us."

Bree glances at me, looking surprised. "I didn't realize we were having an uneasy conversation."

"We're not," I say. "Not exactly. It's just—"

"First, we wanted to congratulate you on Ponderosa Luxury Ranch Resort," Amber says, more masterful than I am at easing in slowly. "It seems like it's really coming together."

"Thanks," Bree says, smiling. "It's a lot of work, but we're getting close."

"So how did you end up with the property, anyway?" I ask. I'm trying to keep my voice casual, but I can tell from the flicker in her eye that my note of judgement came through loud and clear.

"My dad bought the place before I was born," she says. "Had these grand fantasies of being a rancher, but he rarely found time to fly out here."

"You're from the East Coast?" Amber asks.

She nods. "Connecticut. My brothers and I only made it out here occasionally. After our dad died last year—"

"I'm so sorry," Amber says, her brow creasing in a frown. "We'd heard the owner died, but I didn't realize he had children."

"Yes, well, we weren't—close," Bree says carefully. "Anyway, we came out here sometimes when we got breaks at boarding school. My brothers visited more than I did—I think maybe you met Sean?"

"Maybe," Amber says, looking unsure.

"It would have been years ago," Bree says, waving a hand. "Anyway, we inherited the place after our father passed."

"That sounds overwhelming," Amber says.

"In a lot of ways." Bree presses her lips together. "It was a complicated relationship." She clears her throat. "Anyway, we wanted to do something special with the land. Something that honors his memory but also honors the region. We've done a lot of research on the history of the area and some of the Native American influences. Did you know there's a rock outcropping on the east side of the property that used to be a sacred place for the people of the Warm Springs tribe?"

"I didn't," I tell her, a little surprised there's something I don't know about the history of my own backyard. "Are you incorporating that into the theme of the resort?"

"In tasteful ways, where it's appropriate," she says.

"Can you tell us a little more about the resort?" Amber asks. "Most of what we know is hearsay at this point."

"Certainly." Bree folds her hands in her lap. "We're aiming for very high-end clientele. Extremely wealthy, and willing to pay a lot for pampering."

"That sounds—" I stop myself, searching for a word that isn't *horrifying*.

Bree just laughs. "I realize it sounds so snobby when I put it that way, but we basically want to give rich assholes—pardon my language—an opportunity to see the real West." She smiles. "In between massage appointments and golf, of course."

"Of course," Amber says, looking thoughtful. She glances at me, then folds her hands on her lap. "It all sounds really ambitious."

"It is," Bree says. "You should come out for a tour when we're a little closer to finished."

I dig my fingernails into my knees, not sure how much longer I can beat around the bush. "Look, there's something we wanted to talk to you about," I say. "A concern we have."

"Oh?" Bree's expression is neutral, her voice cool.

Amber gives me a smile that says *can it*. "Not a *concern*, so much as a—"

"When did you decide to have country-style weddings out there?" I interrupt. "Because we applied for our event permit six months ago, and the very next week I got word that you guys did the same thing with a remarkably similar-sounding concept."

"Oh. *Oh.*" Bree's brow crinkles. "And you think I stole your idea?"

"No," Amber insists, shooting me a warning look. "But we are trying to figure out whether it's feasible for two properties so close together to execute similar plans."

Bree frowns. "You're thinking there's not room enough for all of us to host weddings?"

I can't tell if that's a challenge in her voice or genuine curiosity. Either way, I'm ready to lay my cards on the table. "The viability of our business plan depends on hosting weddings during the seasons we aren't doing holiday events with the reindeer," I tell her. "We've been planning for years to offer an authentic country wedding destination."

Amber nods and leans forward in her chair. "Mason jars full of daisies, twinkle lights strung up through the rafters, a dance floor in the middle of the barn—"

"—bales of hay for guests to set their plates on when they get up to dance," I add, doing my best to set the scene. "One of the brides we've booked has this great plan to wear her great grandmother's cowboy boots, along with her dress."

"God, your way sounds much better," Bree says.

Her expression is perfectly sincere, and it takes me a second to process what she's saying. "Excuse me?"

Bree shakes her head, looking a little wistful. "We're catering to a different crowd, I'm afraid. Society ladies in Vera Wang gowns and Louboutin heels who want the Cascade Mountains in the background of their wedding photos before they hustle into the air-conditioned ballroom for an eight-course meal that costs more than my car."

I frown at her. "I hate to burst your bubble, but most folks around here don't have that kind of money."

"Exactly," Bree says. "But the sort of families I went to school with do. And they'll think nothing of dropping a couple hundred grand on flying everyone out here for an exotic, destination wedding."

"Central Oregon is exotic?" Amber says.

"To the kinds of people I grew up with it is." Bree smiles. "Look, maybe there's a way we could work together. Our wedding guests will be looking for activities when they get tired of all the spa services and gourmet meals."

"Rough life," I mutter.

"Exactly," Bree says. "So what if we could offer them some sort of real Western experience? Something like reindeer brushing or chicken feeding or fishing in your creek."

I quirk an eyebrow at her, still not buying it. "Pay fifty bucks to shovel manure?"

"You're joking, but guests like ours?" Bree shakes her head. "They'd love it. Anything to pretend they're roughing it. That they're getting a taste of the real West."

I stare at her, wondering if I've misread the whole thing. If I've projected a mean girl where there wasn't one, or maybe just failed to look for the common ground between our two worlds. It wouldn't be the first time in my life I've been too quick to judge.

"That sounds good," I say slowly. "I think maybe we can work with that."

"What about a brainstorming lunch?" Amber suggests. "As soon as the Christmas craziness is done, and you guys get closer to opening. Maybe we can all sit down and come up with ideas for how to work together."

"I'd like that," Bree says, smiling. "Maybe I'll invite my brothers, too."

"Sure." Amber nods. "I'd love to figure out if I remember your brother—Sean?"

"Sean," Bree says. "And James and Mark and—well, I have a lot of brothers.

"I'd love to meet them," I say, surprised to realize I mean it.

"Who knows?" Bree says, giving me a pointed look. "Maybe our cousin, Brandon, could join if we're all getting along nicely and there are no complications."

Her gaze locks with mine, and though it's friendly, there's a warning there that's crystal clear. I stare back, determined not to blink first.

"Absolutely," I tell her. "Sounds great."

CHAPTER 10

BRANDON

"I can't believe you brought me to a restaurant that's not even open yet," Jade murmurs, glancing around in awe. Her gaze travels over the hammered copper bar, the hand-laid slate floors, the colorful Western art on the walls, then back to me. "This place is amazing."

"Stick with me, babe," I joke, lifting my glass of wine. "I'll get you into all the swankiest places."

We're a week from Christmas, and since Jade's been too busy to join me for any official date involving a drive into town, I've arranged something better.

"Is your cousin really a Michelin-starred chef?" she asks.

"Wait 'til you try the first course," I tell her. "Then, you tell me."

As if on cue, Sean shuffles out of the kitchen with two of the most amazing plates of food I've ever seen.

"This is bison steak cured in sake kasu, charcoal onions, and miso eggplant," he says, setting the plate in front of Jade with a flourish. "And this here is the duck confit with spiced carrots, panisse, Greek yogurt, toasted pepitas, and just a hint of tarragon."

"Thank you so much," Jade breathes, looking awestruck as she picks up her fork.

"Thank you for being my test subjects," Sean says. He smiles at her, then slugs me hard in the shoulder before turning and striding back to the kitchen.

"It's a good thing he'll be cooking instead of waiting tables," I tell her. "His people skills could use some work."

"I think he's great," she says as she forks up a bite of the duck. She slips it between her lips and chews, eyes widening in awe. "Oh my God," she says. "This is unreal."

"Told you." I grin and pick up my knife to slice into the steak. Jade finishes her bite of duck before forking up the morsel of buffalo I've just set on the edge of her plate. "Being Sean's guinea pig doesn't suck."

"Were you guys very close growing up?"

I shrug and glance back toward the kitchen. "Not really. My uncle used to bring them out sometimes in the summer to see the ranch and visit us, but it always felt like they came from a different planet."

She nods and takes a sip of her wine. "I met Bree the other day," she says. "She seemed pretty down to earth. A little protective of you, actually."

I laugh and slice off a tender piece of meat. "That sounds like Bree," I say. "She's a great person, though. All my cousins are. And it's been nice to connect with family."

"Do you see your dad very often?"

I nod, recalling my visit a few nights ago. The nurses had parked his wheelchair near a group of residents building a gingerbread house, and the room hummed with cheerful chatter and the tinny buzz of Christmas tunes from a stereo beside an over-decorated tree. I stood watching from a corner, studying the blank look on my father's face.

What was he thinking? Does Christmas make him feel angry, melancholy, or nothing at all? I wish I knew. I wish I could find just one moment of connection.

"I visit a few times a week," I tell Jade now. "More for me than for him. I honestly don't think he knows I'm there at all."

"I'm so sorry, Brandon. Truly." She reaches out and touches my wrist. It's just a light brush of her fingertips, but somehow it feels like a full-body hug.

"For a long time, I blamed my mom," I admit. "For walking out the way she did. For causing my dad's stroke."

"Oh, Brandon." Her voice cracks on the last syllable, and I wonder if I should stop talking.

But this conversation is too important. Getting to know each other like this, with all our clothes on—this matters. To me, to Jade, to what we've been building together. I'm not sure I realized until this moment how true that is.

"Sometimes, I blamed him, too," I admit. "For smoking too much and drinking too much and the fact that all that shit probably contributed."

"To the stroke or your mother leaving?"

"Both." I give a hollow little laugh and rearrange my napkin on my lap. "I guess no matter how you look at it, I didn't have the best role models for health and happiness and relationships."

Jade touches my arm, and this time, she leaves her hand there. "Is that why you've never gotten married?"

The question startles me. From the look on her face, I think it startled her, too.

"I wasn't trying to be nosy—" she begins, but I cut her off.

"You're allowed to be nosy, Jade." I lean a little closer. "We're together, right? Dating? Seeing each other?"

I let those words hang between us, hoping I haven't gone too far. That she sees this as a relationship or something close to it. That we're not just fooling around here.

She takes a sip of wine, and I hold my breath, not sure how to read the guarded look she's giving me.

"Yeah," she whispers at last. "I guess we're seeing each other."

I grin a lot wider than I probably ought to from such a simple answer. "So I don't mind if you ask personal questions." I clear my throat, trying to remember what hers was. "Right. Uh, I guess what happened with my folks probably messed me up for a while. Made me frustrated about Christmas, about relationships —about a lot of things."

"You say that like it's past tense."

"I want it to be," I say. "I'm working on it. You're helping."

Her cheeks redden just a little, and she takes a sip of her pinot gris. "How so?"

"I can't do holiday cheer the way most people spin it," I say slowly. "The Christmas sweaters, the bubbly greetings, the cheesy cards."

She looks at me oddly. "You have something against all that?"

"No, but it's not me. It doesn't click for me the way your ribs did."

"Uh, what?"

I grin and pick up my wineglass. "Your tattoo. The Grinch's heart growing so many sizes it breaks the magnifying glass. That's what I want. What I've been feeling lately."

The flush in her cheeks grows deeper, and she looks down at her plate like she's not sure what to say next. She pokes at a carrot, chasing it around her plate with the tines on her fork. "You have the same effect on me," she murmurs.

When she lifts her gaze again, her eyes seem shimmery. Maybe it's the candlelight, maybe it's the weight of this conversation we've been having. Whatever it is, I feel it, too.

I reach across the table and catch her hand in mine. "What do you say, Jade? Want to be my girlfriend?"

She gives a very un-Jade-like giggle. "Is this like in middle school?" she asks. "Are you going to pass me a note that says, 'will you go with me?' and I have to check the right box?"

"Maybe," I say. "Do you want me to?"

She tilts her head, considering that. "Maybe. I never had that before."

"I'll add that to my to-do list," I promise. "In the meantime, what would you say? Wanna go steady?"

She giggles and dabs a corner of her mouth with her napkin. "Yes," she murmurs, beaming at me from across the candlelit table. "Definitely yes."

* * *

AFTER DINNER IS DONE, I lead her back to my cabin along the snow-lined path I shoveled earlier this evening. The air is icy and crisp and smells like pine, and a faint breeze sends our breath swirling around us in foggy puffs.

"Dinner was amazing," Jade says, gripping my hand a little tighter. "I promise I'll recommend it to everyone I know as soon as the restaurant opens."

"I'm glad you liked it." I let go of her hand a little reluctantly, needing both of mine to unlock the door. I push it open and survey the living room, thrilled to see Bree followed through with the other half of tonight's plan.

"Oh," Jade gasps as she steps over the threshold. She turns in a slow circle, taking in the dozens of candles lining counters and tabletops and little knick-knack shelves on the wall. There's even a candle propped on one of my old football trophies, which Bree must have dug out of storage somewhere.

"It's beautiful," Jade says as she turns back to me. "My God. A fire hazard, but beautiful."

"Don't worry," I assure her. "Bree buys these fancy, expensive fake candles that look just like the real deal. They flicker and look melty and everything, but there's no fire at all."

Jade looks around again, stepping into the center of the living room. I'm used to seeing the space, but I consider it through her eyes. Everything's bathed in a golden light, making the cedar walls glow like embers. Even the caramel-hued leather sofas look luminous in the middle of a red wool rug, basking in the glow of the fireplace. At the other end of the room, the live-edge, lodge-style table is dotted with so many tiny candles that the wood grain ripples like heatwaves.

"So this is how the other half lives." Jade turns to face me. "No wonder you like it here."

"Yeah," I say, closing the gap between us. "Beats the hell out of sleeping on hot sand with a gas mask."

"You did that?"

I nod once. "During a gas attack alert in Iraq, yeah. And in Syria I slept on the iron claddings of a tank to stay warm sometimes."

Jade shakes her head, her expression a little sad. "I'm glad you made it out okay."

"Me, too." It's not just that I'm glad to be alive. I'm glad to be alive right now, in this moment, with Jade. "Did I tell you I put in for the job at the recruitment office in town?"

"No, that's great. I mean—is it?"

"Yeah." I smile. "It means I'd be sticking around. My cousins even agreed to sell me this place for next to nothing if I want it."

"That's terrific," she says. "Can I have a tour?"

"Definitely." I catch her hand in mine and lead her down the hall, trailing my fingers along the cedar railing my cousins finished by hand. "You have to see the bathroom. They're like this in all the cabins we're building."

I draw her into the spacious room and point out the hand-carved stone pedestal sink and the two-headed shower done in hand-laid river rock. "Bree hired a group of artists from the Warm Springs tribe to hand paint the frames on all the mirrors," I explain as I point at one. "The two women who did this one are some of the only tribe members who still speak their native language."

"It's amazing," Jade says, stepping closer to study the artwork.

Geometric slashes of red and black fringe the edges of the mirror, but that's not what I'm looking at. I'm watching the reflection of those lake-blue eyes in the mirror. Seeing Jade's pleasure makes my heart squeeze, and so does the reverence in her voice. "I didn't realize—everything's so beautiful."

"They've paid a lot of attention to detail. And the water system is all LEED certified, so it's very environmentally friendly."

She turns and gives me a small smile. "I didn't know it would be like this," she says. "I guess I pictured something totally different for a rich person's resort."

"I'm glad you like it. They've worked hard out here."

"You, too," she says. "You've been helping, right?"

"Some. I'm mostly just grunt labor. The vision is all theirs."

Jade smiles and reaches for my hand. Her expression has turned coy, and I'm not sure what's on her mind. "So where's the bedroom?"

I grin back and try to ignore the fact that my dick just lunged at the front of my jeans. I'm just glad we're on the same page. That Jade is as glad as I am to finally have this time alone. "Right this way," I say, leading her down the hall. "Did I tell you about my billion-thread-count sheets?"

"You did," she says. "But I really think that's the sort of thing I'll need to experience firsthand to appreciate."

I laugh and pull her into my arms, leaning back against the massive footboard to keep us steady. "And you said you can't flirt."

"I'm working on it," she says. "Learning from the expert."

"In that case, let me show you one of my advanced moves."

She laughs as I grab the hem of her sweater dress, inching it up her thighs as slowly as I can, even though I'm dying to just rip it off. "You're so beautiful, Jade," I murmur as I kiss her. "And mine."

I half expect her to recoil at the possessive chauvinism in my words, but instead, she smiles. "Prove it."

God, I'm really liking Flirty Jade.

I yank the dress up over her head, baring her to me. Tossing it aside, I take in the sight of her standing before me in red satin bra and panties. She's still wearing the tall black boots, and I scoop her up and toss her back on the bed so I can pull them off.

"The zipper is a little tricky," she says, gasping as I kiss my way along the inside of one thigh. "It's on the back of the boot. Careful, they're Amber's."

I growl and tug the zipper on the right boot. "I hope Amber is okay with her boots witnessing what I'm about to do with you."

"What are you about to do?" She grabs hold of my shirt and tugs, pulling it over my head in a tangle of static-filled wool.

"Everything." I strip off the boots and shoulder her thighs apart, kneeling on the floor in front of her. "Everything I've been wanting to do since I first laid eyes on you."

I tug off her panties, dying to taste her again. She gasps as I slide my tongue up the length of her, taking my time reaching her clit. The second I do, she cries out. "Brandon."

I've never heard a woman say my name quite like that, and it sends a fresh surge of need throbbing through me. I circle her with my tongue, loving the way she writhes and gasps under me. I can't get enough of her.

"Please," she pants, digging her fingers into my hair. "Please, Brandon. I want you so much."

This time, I'm prepared. I fumble open the nightstand drawer and pull out a condom. In three seconds, we've got it out of the wrapper and we're rolling it on in the best damn show of teamwork I've ever seen.

I kick my jeans to the floor and slide my body over hers, groaning with the silkiness of her bare flesh against mine. I want to savor this moment. I want to record every sigh, every whisper, every intake of breath as I dot kisses over one breast and then the other.

Jade reaches down between us, more impatient than I am. "I need you inside me," she breathes, urgency glittering in her eyes. "Now, please."

"I love when you beg." I move over her, holding her gaze with mine, breathing her in. Slowly, oh so slowly, I slip inside her, groaning as her slick, snug walls clench around me. "God, you feel amazing."

She moans in response and tilts her head back, baring her throat to my lips and tongue. I kiss her there, savoring the sweetness of her skin and the soft smell of ginger. I start to move, going slowly at first. She's so wet I nearly lose my mind, but I want to savor this. I want to experience every fucking second of it like this is my first time making love to a woman.

In a way, it is. It's not just my first time with Jade. It's my first time with anyone who's made me feel like Jade does. My brain is buzzing, and my body hums with pleasure as I drive into her, then back again. She lifts her hips and meets my rhythm, moving with me as candles flicker on the shelf above the headboard. The room smells like cinnamon and sex, and it's all I can do to keep my head from spinning right off my neck.

"Jade," I gasp, sinking all the way into her before drawing back to do it again.

She arches up against me, urging me on. Her thighs hug my hips and those arms—those glorious, muscled arms—clench firm and strong around me like I knew they would. Her soft little moans in my ear are almost more than I can take. I'm spiraling out of control, and I'm not sure how much longer I can last.

"Oh, God!" she cries out, and bends like a bow. Everything tightens around me at once—thighs, arms, the very center of her—and she unleashes a primal scream.

"Brandon!"

That's all it takes, and I'm chasing her right over the edge, driving into her again and again until we both lie spent on my billion-thread count sheets.

"Come here," I murmur, pulling her against me so I can nuzzle her hair.

Her body is limp and pliable, but she snuggles against me, fitting herself into the crook of my arm like a puzzle piece that's been missing. Her fingertips rest over my breastbone, and several minutes pass before we catch our breath.

"That was—wow," she says.

"My thoughts exactly."

She cuddles closer, then props herself up on one arm to peer down at me. "Can I confess something?"

"As long as it's not an STD."

She smacks me on the chest and rolls her eyes. "Way to ruin the moment, Brown."

"Just going back to what you said the last time we were naked together." I grin and grab the hand that smacked me, planting kisses on each fingertip before resting it back against my chest. "What did you want to confess?"

"I used to think about this," she says. "Back when I was fourteen or fifteen and you were this untouchable, sexy stud I'd see prancing out there on the football field."

"I never pranced."

"Trotted, then." She waves the hand I just kissed, giving me the urge to do it again. "Sashayed. Whatever the hell football players do."

I smile and plant a kiss on her shoulder. "I wish I'd known you then," I admit. "I wish I'd had a chance to be with you."

"I don't," she says. "I can't tell you how glad I am that didn't happen."

"Uh...thanks?"

She smiles and repositions herself so her breast isn't trapped in my armpit. I stroke the tips of my fingers over her shoulder blade, tracing the edges of the delicate wing. "Back then, I wanted you because of what you stood for," she says. "Popularity. Perfection. A chance to feel cool."

"I wasn't that cool."

"It doesn't matter," she says. "Because now, I want you for *you*. For the guy you actually are, instead of the guy in my head."

It is the best thing anyone's ever said to me. Ever, my whole life. My chest tightens like fingers curling into a fist, and several seconds pass before I can get any words out.

"Thank you," I say. "I'm glad, too. That we waited. The version of me you're getting now is a much better guy than the one you would have gotten thirteen years ago."

"Good."

"Not to mention my stamina has improved considerably."

She laughs and falls back onto my chest, snuggling closer. Her breathing slows, and after a few minutes, she goes lax in my arms. I lie there stroking her back for a long time, breathing in the juniper scent of her skin and the gingery scent of her hair and wondering how the fuck I got this lucky.

I'm not sure how long it is before I drift off, but I know we bolt awake at the same time. There's a pounding from somewhere, and it takes me a second to figure out it's in the living room.

"That's the front door." I sit up blurry-brained and rumpled as Jade pulls the sheet around her breasts and blinks at me in the candlelit semi-dark.

"Is it one of your cousins?" she asks.

The front door thunders again. "Jade! It's me, Jade, open up."

"Amber?" Jade leaps out of bed like it's on fire and scrambles to pull the sweater dress over her head. It's inside out and crooked, but she gets her arms through the right holes and is halfway to the door before I've gotten my boxers on.

I'm five steps behind her, thundering through the living room still wondering what the hell is going on. Jade flings the door open, and snowflakes skitter over her bare toes as an icy wall of air knocks me back.

"Amber?" Jade's voice comes out in a rush. "What is it, what's wrong?"

The instant I see Amber's face, I know. I know something awful has happened. There's no color at all in her cheeks, and her eyes are wild with fear.

"Someone left the gate open again," she says. "The gate to the south pasture."

I remember what they said about reindeer and land fidelity. That they won't wander, preferring to stay close to home. I hope to God that's right.

"They don't like to leave, right?" I ask, willing it to be true. "You said they won't get out."

"Right," Amber says, shaking her head. "But other animals can get in."

The words hit me like mortar blast to the chest, and I watch them register on Jade's face.

"Cougar," she whispers. "How bad?"

"Bad," Amber says. "You need to come quick."

CHAPTER 11

JADE

"You're going to be okay, buddy," I whisper. "Just a couple more stitches."

Randy—no stage name yet, since he's just a calf—gives a grunt of displeasure, but doesn't move. The wound is clean and well-numbed, but it can't feel great to have me tugging on his foreleg like this.

On the other side of the fence, his mother paces. Tammy—who's still wearing her halter that says Dasher—stamps a hoof in the dirt and bangs her antlers on the gate. "Don't worry, Mama," I soothe. "We're taking good care of him."

Amber bends low over Randy and strokes the little guy's nose. "Hang in there, sweetie," she whispers. "You're doing great."

Brandon stops pacing behind Amber and moves toward the gate to pet Tammy. She's having none of it. All she wants is to be with her calf. Brandon gives up and returns to my side as I fix the last stitch.

"There." I sit back on my heels and nod at my sister. "You can let go of him now."

Amber stands up and dusts her hands on her jeans. She helps

me set Randy back on his feet, then turns to Brandon. "Thanks for putting that padlock on the gate."

He nods, brow furrowed. "It's a short-term fix. I wish I could do more." He shakes his head, gaze still fixed on Amber. "I can't believe you went after a cougar with a goddamn BB gun. And I thought your sister was a badass."

"My sister *is* a badass," Amber says, shaking her head. "She would have been smart enough to grab the damn .357 instead of the stupid BB gun and actually hit the cougar instead of the trees."

"No one died." I say it to reassure myself as much as anyone, though honestly I'm not sure who I mean. Randy? The cougar? Less death is always a good thing, but right now I'm too terrified to feel grateful.

Randy takes a few timid steps, and I watch his gait to make sure he's moving okay. The sutures are clean and even, and I'm grateful I know what the hell I'm doing when it comes to repairing broken animals. Getting someone else out here at four in the morning would have been impossible, especially when every second counts.

Randy takes a few wobbly steps toward the pen where Tammy paces. His footing seems steady, and I say a silent prayer there's no internal damage. No wounds I can't see. He seems okay, but I want a second opinion.

"Thank God this is the one morning we're closed to the public," I murmur. "I can take him in for x-rays as soon as the clinic opens."

"He looks good," Amber says, her voice a little shaky. "Is it okay to reunite him with his mama?"

I nod. "Yeah. It might even help."

The rising sun glints off Amber's hair as she swings open the gate to the holding pen. Tammy hurries over to greet her calf, nuzzling the side of his face as she inspects every inch of him.

She licks and nudges, snuffing at Randy until she seems satisfied he's okay.

Amber trudges back to my side. "I'm glad it wasn't as bad as I thought."

"And I'm glad you didn't die." I drag her into a forceful hug, my heartbeat slowing for the first time in an hour. "I still can't believe you went after a damn cougar," I growl into her hair. "You could have been killed. What the hell were you thinking?"

My sister shakes her head and pulls back. Tears glitter in her eyes, but she doesn't cry. "I didn't think. I heard the scream, and I had to do something."

"You did good, kid," I tell her. "You saved his life. Probably other reindeer's lives, too."

Brandon clears his throat behind us. "No one else is hurt?"

I shake my head, hardly believing it myself. "Cougars go for the weakest member of the herd." I grit my teeth against an unexpected wave of anger. It's not directed at the cougar, though. "The cougar probably watched for a long time, looking for who was the weakest. Who'd be the best target."

Is that how it was in high school? Did someone spot weakness in me and go for the kill?

You're not weak now. Not anymore.

Sometimes, I'm not so sure.

I turn and begin packing away medical supplies, conscious of Brandon right behind me. "We can't be pissed at the cougar," I mumble. "He was just following instinct. Looking for dinner."

"Right, but that's what we have gates for," Amber says. "And high fences. So they can't treat the herd like a breakfast buffet."

I slam my medical kit shut and stand up. "This is bullshit." I turn to Brandon, conscious of my hands balling into fists at my side. "You're right. Your theory that someone's doing this on purpose? I know you're right."

"I don't want to be right," he says. "I want this to stop."

"So do I."

Amber frowns beside me. "What are you guys talking about?"

"Brandon thinks someone's doing this on purpose," I say. "Someone who wants to hurt us or shut us down or—"

"Who would do something like that?" she demands. She looks at Brandon, and they exchange an uneasy glance.

"I don't know," I say.

Brandon's jaw tightens as he shuffles his feet in the dirt. "What about installing video cameras?"

"How long would something like that take?" I ask.

He rubs a hand over his chin. "Let me make some calls. I've got a cousin who's an electrician."

"Sean?"

"No."

"Bree?"

"No."

"How many damn cousins do you have?"

"Enough," he says, looking grim. "We'll get to the bottom of this, Jade. I promise."

I love that he said "we." That he sees us as a team, and that we're on the same side. He takes a step closer and opens his arms like he's not sure what else to do. I move into them, letting myself sag into an embrace that's warm and solid and comforting. He smells like the hay bale he was sitting on earlier, and I can feel his heartbeat through the thick down of his jacket.

Amber clears her throat behind me. "I'm going to go make some breakfast," she says. "I'll make enough for you and Wonder Boy if you want."

She turns and trudges out of the pasture, her footsteps crunching on frozen wood chips. I close my eyes and breathe in the cedary scent of Brandon's jacket.

"How are you doing?" he asks.

I draw back from the hug, but keep my hands on his chest, not ready to lose contact just yet. "I'm okay. Pretty shaken," I admit. "But it could have been worse."

"So you believe me now," he says. "That someone's doing this on purpose?"

I nod, hating it that he's right. Hating the sour taste in the back of my throat. "Things seemed mostly harmless up until now, but this." I take a hand off his chest and gesture to the pasture. "She could have killed someone."

"She?"

It's not until he repeats the word back to me that I realize what I've said, or that I'm picturing Stacey Fleming's face in my mind.

"Or he," I amend. "It could be anyone."

Brandon's brow furrows, but he lets that pass. "Maybe we should make a list," he says. "Come up with all the names we can think of and then go to the police."

I frown, not sure I like that idea. "That'll make me popular," I mutter. "Going to the cops with a big list of community members I'd like to wrongly-accuse of crimes?"

"It's not a popularity contest, Jade," he says. "It's your livelihood."

"I know that," I tell him. "But my livelihood depends on people not despising me. Or at least keeping the hatred to a minimum so they spend their money out here."

Our voices have grown tense, and Brandon reaches out and brushes a strand of hair from my face. "Come on," he says. "Let's get some food. We can talk about this later."

"Good idea."

We've taken two steps up the path when the crunch of gravel punctures the silence. An engine's rumble grows louder, and I turn to see a big white pickup lurching up the driveway. The logo for Oregon Department of Fish and Wildlife glints on the door panel, and I stare at the ODFW lettering before shifting my gaze to the driver.

Matthew Lerten, a year ahead of me in school. He was one of the sophomores who stole my clay pig, and I wonder if he remembers. I'd heard through the grapevine that he'd been hired by ODFW, but I haven't worked with him. He must be low man on the totem pole to be out here this early, and I brace myself for unpleasant news.

As he slams the truck door and saunters toward us, I'm hit with another flash of memory. Sophomore year. Matthew was a junior by then, and with Brandon already off at basic training, Matthew was the rising star of the school.

I never knew who slid slices of raw ham through the slits of my locker, leaving them to fester over spring break. I only knew the accompanying note that read, "Oink oink!" was scrawled on the same blue notebook paper I'd seen Matthew use in math class.

"Morning," Matthew says.

He's looking at Brandon, not me, and I don't realize my hands are clenched until Brandon reaches for one. I uncurl a fist so he can lace his fingers through mine, but he steps forward to greet Matthew instead.

"Yo, Brown," Matthew calls as he ambles up the driveway with his gaze fixed on Brandon. "Heard you were back in town. Didn't know you were doing this."

I'm not sure what "this" is meant to encompass. The job? Me? I shouldn't leap to judgment, but the memory of festering ham and the fact that Matthew has yet to glance my way sets me on edge. I grit my teeth and order myself not to say anything I might regret.

"You're lookin' good, my man." Brandon says as the two of them exchange one of those complicated male handshakes that ends with body-jarring shoulder slug. "What can I do for you?"

I grit my teeth harder as irritation swells. This is my property, my ranch. There's no reason a Fish and Wildlife officer would show up here to shoot the shit with an old teammate.

Matthew's here for a reason, and it has nothing to do with Brandon.

As though reading my thoughts, Matthew shifts his gaze to me. His frat boy grin turns to a leer, and he gives me the first nod of acknowledgment I've gotten since his arrival. "I need to talk to Jade here," he says. "We've got a problem."

Four words no keeper of exotic livestock wants to hear from ODFW. I force myself to hold eye contact, wondering if it's a help or a hindrance having Brandon here right now. The last thing I want is to look weak. Like the kind of woman who can't handle things herself. I won't give Matthew the chance to smell blood in the water.

I open my mouth to respond, but Brandon beats me to it. "What's the problem?"

Matthew takes his eyes off me, seemingly relieved to deal with his teammate instead. "Well, it seems Jade here hasn't renewed her Non-Native Cervid Holding License with ODFW," he says. "These here Rangifer Tarandus could be a threat to native wildlife, according to ORS 496.021."

He just butchered the pronunciation of every scientific term in that accusation, not to mention rattling off the wrong policy number. But those are the least of my concerns.

"That is absolutely not true!" I glare at Matthew, too annoyed by the false accusation to feign demure innocence. "I sent the forms by certified mail more than three weeks ago."

Brandon glances over at me with a warning look. For what? This is my fucking ranch, my livelihood.

He turns back to Matthew with his nice guy smile pasted in place. "Look, I'm sure there's a reasonable explanation," Brandon says. "Jade's had a few wonky things happening out here on the ranch, and we're actually starting to suspect someone's trying to mess with her. Maybe that's something we should be looking into?"

I grit my teeth, not liking the direction this has just taken.

Matthew adjusts his ODFW logoed ball cap and frowns at me. "That true, Jade? We got more than just a small problem here?"

I know damn well he doesn't care. My relationship with ODFW has been touchy since the first day I filed for permits to open this place. Reindeer aren't like cattle or sheep that authorities know how to regulate, and it's been a learning process for all of us.

I order myself to keep breathing, to speak calmly and rationally. "There's no pro—"

"Actually, Matthew, we're thinking we might need to file a police report," Brandon interrupts. "Maybe you could give us a hand getting the ball rolling?"

I'm so pissed I can't see straight. Who the hell does Brandon think he is? The last thing I need right now is a bunch of cops swarming around this place. In a town this small, gossip spreads like herpes. If locals think there's something wrong with the reindeer or the ranch or *me*, there might as well be. It'll kill our business in the few days left before Christmas.

"Everything's fine," I snap. "Matthew, I have extra copies of the licensing paperwork. I even kept a copy of the certified mail receipt. I'll bring all of it down to the ODFW office as soon as it opens today."

I hope like hell it's that easy. My duplicate copies went missing a week ago, but we should have backups. I'm meticulous about paperwork, and I need Matthew to believe that so he gets the hell off my property.

"I dunno," Matthew says, scratching his chin. "It's past the deadline now. I'm not sure I can—"

"Hey," Brandon interrupts, directing his attention at Matthew. "Did I hear Austin Dugan is the chief of police now?"

"Not yet, but he's up there in the ranks. Sergeant or something." Matthew nods and looks at Brandon again. "You seen him since you got back to town?"

"Nah, but I've been meaning to give him a call." Brandon leans against my fencepost like he's chilling against a bank of lockers after a game, legs stretched out in front of him like he owns the place. "Maybe we can go grab a beer, catch up on old times."

Matthew snorts and gives a mean little laugh. "You remember that time Nolan and me pantsed Ziegler in the locker room?" He hoots with laughter, spittle gathering in the corner of his mouth. "Drake held him down and those two linemen—what were their names?"

"You mean Bollinger and Casey?" Brandon laughs. It's an uneasy laugh, not as booming as Matthew's, but still a laugh. "God, those guys were ruthless."

"Yeah, remember how Pavlock squealed like a little girl when—"

"Look, I'm going to get back to work." My voice breaks through their chatter like a whip crack, and they both snap their attention to me. I straighten my shoulders and stare right back. "You guys can keep doing your little trip down memory lane if you like, but I have things to do." I take a few steps away, but keep my eyes on them. I'm not willing to turn my back. I just want distance between us, a space between me and the brittle laughter that's making my skin itch.

"Aw, c'mon, Jade," Matthew says. "You got a problem with squealing?"

He's baiting me, I know. Reminding me of the Miss Piggy taunts. There's a flicker of confusion in Brandon's eyes, but his shit-eating grin doesn't waver. He's still playing the game, still hell-bent on being chummy with his teammate.

My vision clouds with red, and I blink hard to clear it. "I'll bring by the paperwork later today," I say. "You can show yourself off my property now."

Matthew's expression darkens, and Brandon's isn't too friendly, either. I don't care. And I don't wait for permission to go. I turn and march toward the house, keeping my shoulders square, my head high. Laughter rings behind me, echoing through the pasture. I don't know the source of it, but the sound is like fingernails on a chalkboard.

By the time I reach the house, I'm breathing hard. My heartbeat thunders in my ears, along with the taunting memories.

Look at Miss Piggy go!

Hey, Little Piggy—you want some of this slop?

I'll give you something that'll make you squeal.

Tears streak down my face by the time I get the door open, but I'm too fucking mad to be crying. I swipe the tears away, stomping off snow in the entryway before yanking my boots hard enough to jar an ankle. I kick them aside and march up the stairs in my socks, heels pounding on the battered treads.

"Jade?" my sister calls as I stomp toward the kitchen. "Is that you? I've got Dutch babies in the oven and sausage in the—"

She freezes when she sees my face, her smile dissolving like sugar in a jar of vinegar. "What happened?"

"ODFW," I said. "Matthew Fucking Lerten says we missed the deadline for license renewal. You know damn well I put that paperwork in the mail. You watched me do it."

"You sent it certified, I know." Amber grips her spatula tighter. "What's going on?"

I shake my head, feeling furious and lost and hurt and a whole lot of other emotions I can't possibly name.

"I have no idea, but Brandon's out there yakking it up with him like this is some kind of football team reunion," I growl. "Give them another ten minutes, and they'll be setting up the barbecue out there."

A wave of guilt floods my chest, and I know I might be exaggerating. It's not like Brandon was called upon to take sides. But the sting of shame in my throat is stronger than guilt. Shame I haven't felt for years, not since graduation day. Not since I learned to stand on my own damn feet.

"It'll be okay, right?" Amber asks. "You can fix this."

I don't know if she's talking about the licensing or something else. That *something else* is brewing hot and fierce in my chest. I don't answer her, not sure whether to stay here and problem-solve, or to go upstairs and take a cold shower. Maybe I just need to calm down.

Before I can do anything, a door slams at the front of the house, and footsteps rattle up the stairs. Brandon charges in, looking equal parts annoyed and confused.

"What the hell just happened out there?" he demands. "What got into you?"

"What got into me?" I repeat, blood pressure rising high enough to make my head throb. "Let's see, the guy I'm sleeping with just took the side of some jackass loser from ODFW who's trying to discredit me. That's what got into me."

Brandon stares like he's not sure which part of that to respond to first. "I wasn't taking sides," he says slowly. "I was trying to earn you some good credit with ODFW, since you seemed so determined to be pissy with him."

"I don't need your help, Brandon!" I slam a hand on the counter, wondering how he could be so dense. "And I sure as hell don't need any special favors from your goon squad!"

From the corner of my eye, I see Amber wince. I know I should try to calm down, but I'm too mad right now to do that.

"Look," I tell him. "We're weeks away from Christmas, and the last thing I need right now is trouble with ODFW. I can't risk anything that could jeopardize our ability to operate, or to get the permits I need to take reindeer on the road for events."

Brandon frowns. "And you think being bitchy to Matthew is going to help?"

I smack the counter again. "Well, spilling all our problems to him or to your cop buddy sure as hell isn't!"

"So you're just going to ignore it?"

"No!" I snap. "I'm dealing with it. I've got the paperwork handled, and I'll decide for myself whether to go to the cops and which cop to talk to. I sure as hell don't need your asshole teammates out here—"

"Asshole teammates?" He folds his arms over his chest and stares me down. "You're talking about people I grew up with. Friends of mine. What exactly is your problem with them?"

I glare at him, wondering if he's daring me to say it. If I want to put it out there. "They're a bunch of small-minded jerks, okay?"

"I see," he says slowly. "And is that what you think of me, too?"

I don't respond right away. It's not that I think he's a small-minded jerk. It's that I need to take a few breaths before responding so I calm the fuck down and don't say anything I'll regret.

Amber clears her throat. "Look," she says calmly, clasping her oven mitts in front of her. "Maybe we should all just take a step back and chill. We're in this together, right?"

Brandon glances at her, then snaps his eyes back to me. "I don't know, Jade. Is this a team thing, or are you going to shut me out?"

I drag my hands down my face, torn between wanting to play nice and needing him to know that I won't stand by and let Matthew Lerten or any of the world's bullies rule my life. I don't know what to say. I don't know what to do.

But one thing I do know is that this is all coming at the worst possible time.

"I don't have the bandwidth for this," I say, trying to keep my voice calm. "I'm up to here with Christmas stress right now. I can't breathe or think straight, and I have so much to do I can't sleep. I just—I can't handle this right now, okay? This isn't what I signed on for and—"

It takes me a second to realize Brandon's face has turned to granite. He's staring at me with his jaw clenched, not saying anything at all. He's so quiet even Amber starts to shift uncomfortably.

"I should go," my sister says. "Leave you two alone for a minute."

"No, I should go." Brandon stares at me for two more breaths, his knuckles white where he's gripping the counter. "I think we're done here."

And without another word, he turns and walks away.

CHAPTER 12

BRANDON

Jade's words keep echoing through my head as I drive away.

I'm up to here with Christmas stress...

I can't handle this...

This isn't what I signed on for...

Or maybe they're my mother's words. Almost verbatim what she said more than a decade ago before hurling my father's favorite Christmas snow globe at the wall and storming out the door. I honestly can't tell whose voice is repeating in my brain right now, but I know one thing: Jade King doesn't need me.

She made that damn clear.

I've made it all the way back to Ponderosa Resort before I even realize where I'm headed. Kicking the snow off my boots, I stomp into the lodge and head for the bar. I expect to see Sean there polishing bottles or scribbling recipes. Or maybe Mark measuring lumber for the next batch of tables.

Instead, I spot Bree. She's standing on a ladder with a light in one hand, aiming a camera down at the hammered copper countertop. She stops clicking and looks up at me as I march behind the bar.

"You're welcome," she says from atop the ladder when I don't say anything. "For setting out all the candles last night? I hope it got you laid."

"Not in the mood right now, Bree." I snatch a bottle of whiskey from behind the counter, then hunt for a rocks glass. Where does Sean keep the damn things? Or maybe this is an occasion that calls for swilling straight from the bottle.

I'm still contemplating that when Bree clambers slowly down the ladder. She grabs the bottle from my fist, then uses her free hand to whack the back of my head.

"What the hell is your problem?" she demands.

I make a feeble grab for the bottle, but she's quicker and feistier than I am.

"None of your business," I grumble.

I know I'm being an asshole, but I can't seem to stop.

"The hell it's not my business." Bree slams the bottle onto the counter, then jams her hands onto her hips and levels me with a death-glare that would make my former drill sergeant's nuts shrivel. "You come storming in here like someone ran a rake over your testicles, and now you think it's a good idea to start chugging whiskey? You of all people know that's the dumbest thing you could do."

She has me there. I'm being an idiot in more ways than one, and she has every right to call me on it. Defeated, I retreat to the opposite side of the bar and sink empty-handed onto one of the leather-topped stools.

After a few seconds, Bree walks around the bar and sits down beside me. She stretches an arm over the bar, grabs a bowl of maraschino cherries, and pushes them in front of me.

"Here," she says. "I was using them in a photo, but you need them more than I do."

I look up at her. "Maraschino cherries?"

"You loved these as a kid. Remember?"

"I remember." I'm touched that she would, given how little

time we spent together. She used to sneak them out of the wet bar where her father made his manhattans, giggling as we scurried away with cherry juice dribbling down our chins.

I ignore the cherries and glance at my cousin, wondering how much she knows about my upbringing. The fact that she knew about my dad's drinking tells me it's more than I realized.

"So," she says. "Want to tell me what happened?"

"Not really."

"Yes. You do."

I hate her for being right again, but not as much as I hate myself right now. I hesitate, not sure how much to share. How much to let her in.

"I don't think things are going to work out with Jade."

She stares at me. "Tell me you didn't bone someone else."

"Of course I didn't bone someone else," I bark. "What kind of asshole do you think I am?"

"Not that kind," she says, her expression coolly smug. "But I wanted to hear you say it."

"Fuck." I let out a slow breath and clasp my hands together on the bar, sinking my head down onto them.

A touchy-feely sort of cousin might pat me on the back.

Bree shoves the bowl of cherries against my arm. "Have one. It'll help."

I look up as she jostles the bowl again, making the little red orbs wobble like superballs. I grab one and shove it in my mouth, mostly to get her to shut up about the damn cherries.

"Hell," I mumble as I chew. "You're right." Something about a mouthful of obscenely-sweet fruit makes it harder to stay pissed.

"I'm right about telling someone, too," she says. "You'll feel better if you talk about what happened."

"I hate you," I mutter, the exact opposite of the truth.

"I know," she says, and I'm pretty sure she does.

So I start at the beginning. Not just what happened with Jade, but my parents' split. My mixed feelings about Christmas. Hell, I even tell her about the scene with my teammates at the burger joint last week. I don't know why, but it's like someone pulled the cork from a wine bottle, and all the sticky, bitter contents have come glugging out.

Bree listens quietly, her eyes steady on me. A few times she nods or shoves the cherries at me again, but mostly she just listens. I'm not sure I've ever had anyone pay such rapt attention while I pour my guts out like I'm confessing to a goddamn priest.

She waits until I'm finished before asking a single question. "Do you love her?"

It's not the question I expected. I consider playing dumb, but there's no point. I pick at a cherry stem, uncertain how to answer. "I'm not sure I know what love is."

"That's bullshit, and you know it." Bree folds her hands on the counter and stares at me. "You're one of the most loving guys I know. You've done more work around this place than any of us, even though we're not paying you a dime."

"You're family."

"That's love, dumbass."

"Yeah," I mutter. "I'm really feeling the love."

Bree shakes her head. "I've watched you with those kids who think you're Santa. The kindness and patience and sweetness you show them? That's love, too."

"That's a job."

"Jesus Christ." Bree elbows me hard in the ribs. "You visit your father day in, day out, even though he has no idea who you are. That's love, asshole."

My throat feels thick and raw, and I force myself to swallow before speaking. "I don't know that I'm capable of the other kind of love," I tell her. "The kind with Jade."

"You are." Her voice has softened, and she gives me such an earnest look that I'm tempted to look away. "But there's something you should know about loving a woman like Jade."

"What are you talking about?" I mutter. "You met her, what —once?"

"Let's just say I recognize a kindred spirit when I see one." Bree presses her lips together, and I can tell she's weighing her words carefully. "Girls who spend their formative years being picked on or bullied or beaten down. Girls who grow up vowing they'll never, ever stand for that shit again."

I stare at her, taken aback not just by her words, but by the passion in them. The specificity. "You got all that out of a fifteen minute meeting?"

"I got it because I was that girl, too, Brandon," she says. Her eyes are tearless, but her voice sounds heavy, like she's talking through wet wool. "I know what it feels like to be ostracized for being different. Too short, too tall, too fat, too skinny." She waves a hand, and the expression she gives me is almost pitying. "I asked around about Jade. Folks in town filled me in."

"About what?"

"About the fact that kids bullied the shit out of her for being chubby. Or for being different. A farm kid or whatever."

I stare at her, wondering if this is true. I remember my ex-classmates at the burger joint, how they seemed more familiar with Jade's past than I was. And I remember what Stacey told Sean. Was it worse than I imagined? Did I miss something that big?

A flash of memory bowls into me like a St. Bernard lunging for a steak. "The pig."

Bree narrows her eyes at me. "What did you say?"

I love that she's coiled and ready to jump to Jade's defense, but I hold up my hands. "No, that's not what I meant."

I shake my head, buying myself some time as my memory clouds with visions of a high school hallway filled with garish florescent light. A bunch of second-string linemen—sophomores, maybe juniors—tossing a lumpy clay pig as a girl in plaid flannel runs between them, round cheeks streaked with tears.

I look at Bree as my gut churns. "I do remember Jade."

Only it's not the same Jade I know now. Or maybe it is. Maybe I've been so stuck in my own head that I've failed to see the whole picture of Jade. I saw the heart, but not the hurt. I saw the toughness, but not the things that made her that way.

"Your friends," Bree says. "Your football buddies or cheerleaders or whatever. Were those the kids who made her life hell?"

I nod, though I'm not totally sure. I remember Matthew Lerten, his smug face sneering down at the girl as he held the pig overhead.

Or as he held the stupid paperwork over her head this morning.

"I'm such an asshole."

Bree doesn't argue, but she does pat my hand. "Kids are fucking mean," she says softly. "They'll crucify anyone who's different. I know guys like you don't always see it. Nice guys at the top of the food chain rarely look down. You're too busy clinging to your own rungs on the ladder. But girls like me, like Jade—that shit lives with us for a long damn time."

I fist my hands on the bar as her words sink in. Why didn't I do more to help? To notice what others were going through. I'm not sure whether to feel more protective of Bree or Jade right now, but I know I want to punch anyone who ever made either of them feel bad about themselves.

"I'm sorry," I say.

"Why?" she asks. "Were you a bully?"

I shake my head, but the denial does nothing to alleviate my guilt. "I wasn't, but I could have done more to notice it. To jump in and help if that shit was going on."

"Pity is the worst thing you can offer up now," she says. "Respect. That's what we want. What we need."

I stare at my hands, replaying this morning's interaction with Jade. The way she stood up to Matthew, to me. How long did it take her to get strong enough to do that?

"There's no one I respect more than Jade," I murmur. "She's smart and kind and clever and strong and beautiful and—"

"So tell her all that," Bree says. "Tell her now, before she finds another Santa." She lifts her chin as she reaches across me to grab a cherry. "Or another man to warm her bed."

Those words make my chest ache so badly I can't breathe. God. The thought of Jade with anyone else is like an icicle slipped between my ribs. Bree's right. I have to talk to Jade. I have to make this right.

I snatch my phone and dial her number, surprised to discover my hands are shaking. It rings once, twice, then goes straight to voicemail.

"This is Jade King at Jinglebell Reindeer Ranch—"

"The reindeer calf," I say, hitting the button to end the call. "She's taking him to the vet."

Bree frowns. "Which vet?"

"I don't know." I set my phone on the bar. My heart is racing as my brain reels with different scenarios. Different ways to win her back, to say I'm sorry.

None of them play quite right in the exam room of a veterinary clinic.

A decade.

Maybe more.

That's how long Jade has carried this burden. How long she's felt the sting of hurtful words and held the knowledge of how shitty people can be to each other.

How long have I done the same thing?

I swallow hard, and look at my cousin. Bree's eyes are clear and calm, and I know she'd approve of what I'm going to do next. What I need to do, before I can make things right with Jade.

"I need to see my dad."

* * *

The smell of antiseptic and tapioca pudding rush me like linebackers as I push through the doors of the Central Oregon Dementia Care Unit. The commingled scent is as familiar as the ugly green and white tiles on the floor, and I focus on keeping my breathing steady as I head toward my father's room.

Making my way down the hall, I shift the duffel bag I'm carrying from one hand to the other. I'm greeted by two nurses whose names I've forgotten, but whose faces are vaguely familiar. I'm pretty sure I dated at least one of them in high school, though never more than twice.

I hope I wasn't an asshole. I hope I was kinder to them than other guys were to Jade or Bree.

"Hi, uh—Jean," I try when a third nurse gives me a flirty little finger wave.

"It's Jen," she says. "But nice try. Your dad's awake; you can go on in."

"Thanks. And, uh—sorry."

She hesitates, but doesn't ask what for. "Don't mention it." Her eyes are filled with more kindness than I deserve, and I make a mental note to pick up Christmas cookies for the staff.

I move through the doorframe of my dad's room, feeling gangly and awkward in my own skin. He's sitting in the corner by the window like always, staring out into the dull afternoon light. There's something in his hand, and it takes me a moment to realize it's the Santa hat.

"Hey," I say softly.

He doesn't look up, which is normal. But I notice his fingers working the white fur on the edge of the hat, stroking and petting like it's an animal he's soothing.

I step into the room and pull a chair up beside him. Setting my duffel bag at my feet, I sit down next to him and hesitate a moment before putting a hand on his knee. "Pop?"

Again, he doesn't look. But his hands go still on the red velvet edge of the Santa hat.

"There's something I want to tell you," I say. "Something I should have said a long time ago."

Silence. Outside, a flutter of snowflakes swirl in a wind gust.

"I know it's too late now, but I want you to know I don't blame you," I say softly. "That it wasn't your fault Mom left."

His palm moves again, stroking the length of red velvet all the way to the white fur trim. He doesn't look at me, and his eyes are cloudy as he stares out over the snow-crusted lawn.

"Anyway, I wanted you to know that," I say. "I don't blame you, and I don't blame Mom, and I don't even blame—" my throat clogs again, and I fight to swallow back the lump. "I don't blame Christmas."

This time, his eyes flicker. I'm sure of it. Slowly, so very, very slowly, he turns to face me. His eyes are rheumy, but they lock with mine and hold for a few breathless seconds. He blinks once —acknowledgement of something, or just a biological function?

His fingers stroke the fur trim again, petting and pulling at it. I point to the hat.

"You want to wear it?" I ask. "Would you like me to put it on you?"

No response, not verbal anyway. But his hands go still again.

"I have one just like it," I tell him. "A beard, too. Want to see?"

I don't wait for a response this time. I just slide my hand into the black duffel bag at my feet. I sit up and fix the snowy-white facial hair to my chin, then don the hat.

When I meet my dad's eyes again, one corner of his mouth is tilted up. It's faint, but it's there. I wouldn't call it a smile, exactly, but it's the closest I've seen years.

"Here." I slide the Santa hat off his lap, ready to stop if he grabs hold of it or seems upset. But he doesn't.

Carefully, I arrange the hat on his head. It's lopsided and the tassel bops against his forehead, so I straighten it out before sitting back to admire the effect. He stares at me. I stare back, my chest tight and sore.

"You look great, Pop." My voice is gravelly, and my eyes are stinging.

The edge of his mouth tugs again, even closer to a smile. Then he gives an almost infinitesimal nod.

He's the first to break eye contact. His gaze skids sideways, and for a moment I think I've lost him. That he's gone back to staring sightlessly at the frosty garden outside.

But, no, he's staring at a book. It's sitting on the edge of his dresser, so I reach out and pick it up. As I study the tattered cover, recognition washes over me like a salty wave.

"*How the Grinch Stole Christmas*," I read before glancing at my father. His expression is neutral, but my heart is pounding in my chest. "Where did you get this?"

No response, but I'm used to that by now.

"I had this when I was a kid," I say. "I recognize the cover. And this little dent on the corner from when I dropped it on the floor. You used to read this to me."

My father's hands twitch in his lap as he stares back. There's something in his eyes—a question? A request?

"You want me to read it to you?" I ask softly.

His head barely moves, but I swear it's a nod. Even if it's not, I know what to do. I reach out and squeeze his hand. We sit there for a few silent moments like that. Just two broken guys in Santa hats, doing our best to put the past behind us.

Then I draw my hand back, open the book, and begin the story.

IT'S GROWING dark by the time I finally drive back to Jingle Bell Reindeer Ranch. The sky has the purplish cast of a bruise, and stars are just starting to prick through the ink.

I'm not sure yet what I'll say to Jade, but I'm hoping the words come to me. I know one of them will be "sorry." Another might be "love," though I'm not sure she'll want to hear it. She may well hate me for all I know.

I cut my lights as I pull into the parking area, but not before a dark shape catches my eye. At first, I think it's a reindeer. One of the bigger ones like Donner or Cupid, whose real names I can never keep straight.

It *is* a reindeer, I realize as I step out of the truck.

But it's more than that.

I grab my Maglite from the truck and flick it on, then start up the path toward the barn. The image gets clearer as I approach, and I train my beam on the two figures up against the barn.

One of them is Tammy, whose name I recall is Dasher. She's facing the side of the barn, her massive, branchlike antlers pressed against the building like toppled coatracks.

Pinned between them is a man. A man holding a gas can, looking helplessly toward me as I approach.

I quicken my pace, though it's clear the guy isn't going anywhere. Tammy is making damn sure of that. Her eyes roll to glance at me, but she doesn't move her head. I stare at the man for a moment, taking it all in.

"Evening," I say at last.

His throat moves as he swallows. "It's not what it looks li—"

"Shut up."

I pull out my phone and snap two photos. Then I dial Jade's number. It rings once, twice, three times, and I'm afraid it will go to voicemail again.

When she picks up, her voice is calm, but breathless. "Yes?"

"Jade," I say.

Saying her name feels wonderful, so I say it again, nearly forgetting why I've called. It's so good to hear her voice. "Jade, there's something you need to see."

She pauses, and I wonder if I've caught her in the middle of something. Watching Christmas specials or stringing popcorn garland or, hell, interviewing a replacement Santa.

The thought makes my gut churn, or maybe that's the scene in front of me. I still can't fucking believe what I'm looking at.

"Brandon, I don't think it's a good idea to—"

"Come outside," I tell her. "Please. And bring Amber."

CHAPTER 13

JADE

I approach the barn with my heart thudding like a jackhammer and an apology ringing in my ears. I don't know why Brandon wants to talk out here, but I'm game for meeting him anywhere. I'd join him at a slaughterhouse if it meant I got the chance to say I'm sorry.

"Why are you bringing me?" Amber whispers. She blows on her gloved hands as she trudges beside me, boots crunching in the snow. "Shouldn't you do this alone?"

"He asked for you," I tell her. "Maybe he wants a witness in case I flip out again. Or maybe he wants to talk about—*oh*."

All my words, all my theories vanish as my eyes land on the scene beside the barn. Brandon stands with a flashlight beam trained on Tammy. She's facing away from him, the outside tines of her massive antlers pressed against the barn to form a sort of makeshift prison cell.

A cell that currently contains one miserable-looking photographer.

"Zak?" Amber steps forward, brow furrowed in confusion. "What's going on here?"

Brandon toes a gas can on the ground at Zak's feet. "Want me to take a guess?" he asks. "Or you want me to just tell you what my cop buddy shared a second ago when I texted him a photo of this?"

"A police officer was out here taking fingerprints off the south gate this morning." I stare at Zak, who has the good sense to stare at his feet. "I have a hunch I know whose they are."

Amber takes two more steps forward and rests a hand on Tammy's neck. That makes two furious-looking females with their eyes trained right on Zak. "What the hell is going on here?"

"Babe," he says. "I can explain."

"No, you can't." Amber shakes her head. "Not to me, anyway. To the police, maybe."

Zak shoots a pleading look at Brandon. "Help me out here, man," he says. "You know what it's like to do stupid shit over a woman."

"You're right there," Brandon says, and my heart does a funny little lurch. "But you passed stupid a few miles back and headed down the road to certifiably nuts."

"What the hell are you talking about, anyway?" Amber demands. "How does screwing up our farm—"

"—and their website," Brandon adds.

"—and our ODFW paperwork," I add. It's a guess, but I can tell from the flush in Zak's cheeks it's the right one. How many times has he ducked into my office to recharge camera batteries? And I'm ninety-five percent sure he has a sister who works for the post office.

"All of that is beside the point," Amber says. "How on earth would any of that help you out?"

Zak tries to move, but Tammy stomps a hoof in the dirt at his feet. She shifts her head a few inches, bringing her sharper eye-guard tines within inches of Zak's throat. Her antlers are much too long for him to reach out and grab her halter, but one of us could do it.

We could, but we choose not to. The reindeer headlock is

working just fine.

"Did you do all of that, Zak?" I demand.

He doesn't answer right away, which is fine. I'll leave it to the cops to question him properly.

"Look, Amber and I were supposed to get married," he mutters.

My sister stares at him. "We were?"

Zak gives an exasperated snort. "Well, we would have," he snaps. "We were on our way to that point before you got this crazy idea to open a reindeer ranch. If it weren't for this stupid farm and these stupid reindeer and—gah!"

Tammy shifts again, all four-hundred pounds of her pressing forward. I don't know if she's pissed about Zak's words or the role he played in harming her calf. Could be that dinner's a little late.

"Look," Zak gasps. "I wasn't trying to hurt anyone. I just thought if Amber realized this whole thing was a bad idea, she'd come back, and we could pick things up where we left off."

"I can't believe you did this." Amber shakes her head, and I can tell she's in that zone between hurt and fury. That place where you're too damn angry to cry. "I trusted you," she chokes out. "And you risked my family, my livelihood, my *animals*—"

Tammy moves again, and it's enough for Zak to see an opportunity. He ducks between the tines of her antlers and takes off running, his boots slipping in the snow as he tears across the paddock toward the gate.

"Stop!" Brandon takes off after him, more sure-footed in the slush than Zak is. Zak bobs left, then right, zig-zagging across the pen. But he's no match for Brandon's speed and power, and definitely no match for a guy who knows how to tackle.

Down they go, a tumble of limbs and curse words, with Brandon landing on top of Zak in an undignified heap.

"Get off me!" Zak grunts.

"No way."

The two men flail as Amber and I hurry toward them with Tammy right behind us. While there's no longer any question what sort of guy Zak is, I'm still dismayed to see he fights dirty. Turning his head to the side, he bites Brandon's arm.

"Son of a bitch!" Brandon yelps.

Zak struggles again, nearly tipping Brandon off his body.

A gunshot cracks the inky night. Everyone freezes.

I turn to see my sister holding the .357 overhead, its snub nose aimed at the sky. She draws it down like a goddamn gangster, and I half expect her to blow smoke from the barrel. She turns and looks at me.

"I grabbed the right gun this time," she says.

I nod and stare at her. "Yeah, you did."

"Jesus," Zak sputters, and I turn to see him spit dirt out of his mouth. "You're all fucking crazy."

"Ha!" Amber stomps through the slushy bark until her boots are inches from his face. Tammy follows behind like a bodyguard with antlers. "That's rich, coming from the asshole who thought he could win a woman by ruining her life."

She's not pointing the gun at him, but she's still holding it. Zak's gaze stays fixed on the muzzle, and he seems to rethink the idea of saying anything else.

Brandon looks at me, then at Zak, then Amber. "I don't think he's going anywhere."

He heaves himself off Zak and stands up, brushing dirt off his jeans.

"Fucking rent-a-cop," Zak mutters. "Running around here like a 'roided out security guard."

"Good, since that's what I hired him to do," Amber snaps. "And I wouldn't have had to if it weren't for you and your bullshit, Zak." She turns to me and frowns. "Um, sorry."

I look at my sister and wonder why I'm not more surprised. "You asked Brandon to be Security Santa?"

She nods, looking sheepish. "Are you mad?"

I shake my head, flooded with a hundred different emotions, but none of them anger. "It's okay," I tell her. "We needed help. And I needed to pull my head out of my butt."

A disco flutter of red and blue lights dances across the pasture, and we all turn to see a police cruiser coming up the driveway. Brandon must have summoned them, or maybe it was the gunshot. Instead of feeling annoyed, I'm filled with gratitude.

"Brandon," I whisper, turning back to him. I need to get the words out fast before we have company. "I'm so sorry about our conversation this morning. The things I said to you. I was hurt and lashed out and—well, anyway. Can you forgive me?"

"Forgive you?" He shakes his head, looking genuinely baffled. "What on earth for?"

"For being a bitch," I say. "For not giving you a chance to help when that's all you were trying to do."

"No, Jade, I'm sorry." He steps forward and takes my hand. "You had every right to be upset. I understand why you felt disrespected and threatened and—well, you shouldn't feel that way on your own property. Or anywhere, ever."

He's looking at me like he wants to say more, and I wonder what it is. I wonder if he knows about high school, about why Matthew's words poked and pinched like barbed wire around my heart. Something tells me he does. Something tells me we'll have time to talk about it later. To spread our stories out on the kitchen table and exchange them like Christmas cards.

"It's okay," I tell him. "I can stand up for myself."

"I know you can." He squeezes my hand. "And I'm so damn proud of you for that."

I shake my head, still needing to apologize. "I could have been more tactful," I tell him. "And I definitely shouldn't have taken it out on you."

"No, Jade—couples argue. It happens. It was a simple disagreement we could have resolved like adults. I'm the one who stomped out of here like a toddler having a tantrum. That's not me. I can promise that won't be me ever again if you give me a chance to prove it."

He takes my other hand, and we stand there with our gloved fingers interlaced as lights from a second cop car dance across the snow. It's the sheriff's department this time, and I can't help wondering how they got here so fast.

But that's not what I care about right now. I meet Brandon's eyes again and swallow hard. "I definitely believe in second chances," I say. "For both of us."

"Good," he says. "Because I love you. I love you, and I want to make this thing work between us."

Something pings through my chest like a lightning bolt going off in a hay field. Tears sting my eyes, and I squeeze Brandon's hands so hard I hear a knuckle pop.

"I love you, too," I breathe. "So much."

"Oh, puke," Zak grumbles.

"Shut up!" Amber snaps, pointing the pistol at him.

Beside her, Tammy bends her knees in a slight squat and offers proof of our commitment to ensuring the livestock are well-hydrated. Rivulets of reindeer pee trickle through the snow-caked dirt in a direct path toward Zak's head.

"Gah!" he grunts and tries to roll away.

My sister plants her boot on his chest and waves to the cops trudging toward us through the pasture. "Over here! Hurry!"

I turn back to Brandon, breathless in the cold air. "I love you," he says again. "So much."

"Me, too."

As far as romance goes, it leaves something to be desired. My toes are frozen, and we're standing in barn muck and reindeer pee while my sister holds a gun on her ex. This isn't the love scene of my youthful fantasies.

Somehow, it's better.

And as Brandon draws me into his arms, I can't think of anyplace I'd rather be.

EPILOGUE

BRANDON

I toe off my boots in Jade's entryway and set them by the door. Silently, so I don't wake anyone, I tiptoe sock-footed up the stairs toward the second floor.

It's ten minutes to midnight on Christmas Eve, and I'm not even sure Jade's still up. But she asked me to come tonight, no matter how late, so we could wake up together on Christmas morning. I'm later than I'd planned, thanks to an evening spent watching the old Rudolph cartoon with my dad—three times through, at his urging—but I've made it before midnight.

I follow the scent of gingerbread to the kitchen, where Jade stands at the counter pressing little decorations into still-warm cookies. She looks up and smiles as I walk into the room, and I seize the chance to steal a cookie.

"Ooh, they're reindeer," I say, pausing to admire the cutout shape before biting off its head. "Pretty tasty," I mumble around a mouthful of crumbs.

"You goober, those are for the reindeer." She snatches the cookie out of my hand and sets it back on the tray, where I get a closer look at the cookies.

"They're made with high-cellulose orchard hay meal for

fiber," Jade informs me. "Plus rehydrated beet pulp pellets for protein and minerals."

I study the reindeer shapes, wavering between curiosity and nausea. "What's that on top?"

"Little bits of lichen," she says. "Their favorite treat."

I grab a paper towel from the dispenser and wipe my tongue with it, grinning in spite of myself. "I love that you baked Christmas cookies for the reindeer."

I love a lot of other things about her, too, which I've been making the effort to tell her every single day. "Are you at a stopping point?" I ask. "I have something for you."

"Oooh, presents?" She grins and sets down the little dish of greenish pellets she's been holding. "I have one for you, too. I'll go grab it and meet you in the living room."

I watch her scurry out of the room, admiring the curve of her hips and the way her hair trails behind her as she twirls around the banister and up the stairs.

Mine, I think.

The thought warms me all the way through. I turn and head toward the living room, where Jade and Amber have set up the family Christmas tree. Ornaments from their childhood dangle from each branch, and I stoop to admire a lumpy star made of play-dough. Beside that is a tarnished silver ornament with a family photo in the center, and I peer at the image of Jade and Amber as pigtailed grade-schoolers sandwiched between two beaming grownups. The parents are flying from Hawaii in the morning, since Christmas-day flights are cheaper. I can't wait to meet them.

"Here we go," Jade announces as she bounds into the room in stocking feet. She's holding a gift-wrapped package the size of a thin paperback, and I follow her to the overstuffed sofa beside the tree.

"Mind if I tuck my feet under you?" she asks as we cozy up together.

"Not at all. Mind if I ask if you're wearing a bra?"

She gives a gasp of mock indignation, but I can tell from her smile she's not offended.

I can also tell she's not wearing the bra, but I want to hear her say it.

"You said that was your Christmas wish, right?" she says. "Snuggling beside the tree with Christmas carols on the stereo and a braless babe beside you."

She grins and jerks a thumb toward the stereo, which is playing her favorite Barenaked Ladies Christmas album. I grin back like the lucky bastard I am and lean close for a kiss, skimming my thumb over her breast through the thin fabric of her t-shirt.

"You make all my wishes come true," I tell her.

It sounds cheesy, but it's honest to God true.

Jade smiles and points to the package she's handed me. "Open it."

I tug at the edges of the tape, not sure if I'm supposed to save the wrapping paper or rip into it. Jade seems like a save-the-paper kind of girl, so I take my time peeling back the edges and unfolding the red and green wrapping from the hard shape inside.

The metal edges of a photo frame come into view, and I hold it in my palms for a few silent seconds, staring at the image. It's me at seventeen years old, football helmet under one arm, hand raised for a high five.

Beside me, with his own palm clapped against mine, is my father.

The image is grainy and a little out of focus, but his eyes are clear and bright, and his smile is so broad it takes up his whole face.

"Where on earth did you find this?" I breathe.

"Zak," she says, sounding a little embarrassed. "I know it's weird, since he's in jail right now for trying to burn down our ranch and—"

"It's amazing."

"It is, isn't it?" Jade shifts her weight so her toes curl under my leg and her breast brushes my arm. "Amber dug it out of a box of pictures Zak took in high school. His mom was going to throw the whole thing out, but Amber found this."

"I can't believe it," I murmur. "This has to be one of the last pictures of my dad and me together before his stroke."

She beams, looking relieved. "I'm glad you like it. I was worried about dredging up old memories, but you both look so happy here."

I touch the side of her face, so in love with her I'm almost dizzy with it. "Sometimes it's good to dredge up old memories," I tell her. "It's how you make things better moving forward."

She smiles and turns her head to plant a kiss in the center of my palm. "I couldn't agree more."

She doesn't need to say anything else. Over the last week, we've spent many late nights sharing our stories. About high school and family and past and present and future. I could never get tired of holding her in my arms and talking until we both fall asleep.

I grip the photo frame tighter in my hands. "It's perfect," I tell her. "Thank you."

I can't stop staring at the image. My throat is thick with emotion, and I'm blown away by the magnitude of this gift. By the thought that went into it.

"I love it," I say, tearing my eyes off the photo to look at Jade. "And I love you."

"I love you, too." She grins. "Did you say you had something for me?"

I nod. "Yeah. I do."

I set the photo on the coffee table and slide a hand into my jacket pocket. The envelope I withdraw is faded and torn on one corner. Jade's expression is curious, probably wondering why the hell I'm giving her a beat-up, used greeting card when she gave me such a thoughtful present.

I flip over the envelope and turn it so she can read the name on the front of the card.

Brandon.

Her eyes jerk to mine and then go wide. It's not the name that startled her. It's the handwriting. The fact that she recognizes it as her own.

She opens her mouth, but no sound comes out.

"It's yours, right?" I ask. "You slid it in my locker my senior year?"

Slowly she nods and draws a hand to her mouth. "How did you—where did you—oh my God."

She takes the envelope and draws the card out slowly. The envelope is tattered and soft with age, and she holds the Christmas card gently like an injured butterfly.

A smile warms her face as she reads the front of the card. I know the words without looking, and the image is burned into my brain. A cartoon Santa in the back of his sleigh, gesturing with exasperation as a lone reindeer snoozes beside the rest of the team.

"Oh, great—a flat!" read the words on the front of the card.

But that's not why I kept it all these years.

Jade opens the card, her eyes moving back and forth as she reads the words inside. When she lifts her gaze to mine, those blue lakes are filled with tears.

"You're one of the good ones, Brandon Brown," she whispers. "You knew I wrote that?"

I shake my head. "No. Not until a few days ago when I saw your handwriting and made the connection."

"But how did you—why—" She stops and takes a breath. "I can't believe you kept it all these years. An anonymous Christmas card from a stranger?"

"Because it meant something to me," I say. "The week you slid that card in my locker was the same week my mom left."

"Oh my God." She covers her mouth with her hand. "I had no idea."

"No one did." I swallow hard, aching to get out the rest of the words. "But seeing these words you wrote—that someone saw me as one of the good guys. It meant something to me."

"And you kept it all these years."

I nod. "It went with me on all my tours. Iraq, Syria—"

"I can't believe this."

I move my arm to the back of the couch, wanting to touch her hair. To be close enough to feel her body soft and warm and pressed against mine. "It was a reminder that someone saw something good in me," I tell her. "Something besides the touchdowns and the military honors and the jock reputation. Something in *me*."

A tear slips down her cheek, and I reach out to catch it with my thumb. Jade smiles and sets the card down in her lap. Then she stretches up to put her arms around my neck. "I love you so much, Brandon," she murmurs against my neck. "You *are* one of the good guys."

"I love you, too." My throat cinches up like there's a hot rubber band inside, but I swear to God I've never been this happy in my whole life.

I don't tell her about the other gift. Not yet. The engagement ring is tucked safely back at my cabin, waiting for the time a few weeks or even months from now when it's a saner moment to propose. I don't want to scare her off, but I know without a doubt she's the woman I'm meant to spend the rest of my life with.

I just need to give her time to reach that same place.

"Merry Christmas, Jade," I murmur.

"Merry Christmas." She draws back and gives me a smile

that's tipped with mischief. "So," she says. "You brought the Santa costume like I asked?"

"You ditched the bra," I tell her. "It seems fair I should honor your Christmas request."

"Good." She grins wider. "I was thinking you could put it on later. And maybe I could sit on your lap."

I laugh and pick up the card, then set it carefully atop the picture frame on the table. "Oh yeah?" I scoop my hands under Jade, earning myself a startled squeal. She giggles as I pull her onto my lap and snuggle her close against my chest. "Maybe we should practice now?"

"Yeah?"

"Yeah." I plant a kiss along her hairline, and another at the edge of her mouth. "And maybe we can talk about the first thing that pops up."

She throws her head back in laughter, and I seize the chance to draw a long trail of kisses through the hollow of her throat. "Merry Christmas, Jade."

"Merry Christmas, Brandon."

***

Ready to read Amber and Sean's story? That's next in the Ponderosa Resort Romantic Comedy Series, and I'm excited for you to see how they find their way to each other in *Chef Sugarlips*. Keep scrolling for an exclusive sneak peek at the first chapter...

https://books2read.com/b/3L0aqw

YOUR EXCLUSIVE SNEAK PEEK AT CHEF SUGARLIPS

AMBER

"Picture a bunch of twinkle lights in those rafters, and the hay bales over there would be the edge of the dance floor."

I deliver my most charming smile to the bride and groom before zeroing in on the mother of the bride. She beams like I've handed her a puppy and a vodka-laced Frappuccino, and I'm positive I am currently her favorite person in this barn.

I have that effect on moms.

But it's the bride who needs convincing, so I turn back to her. Julia's blonde hair is arranged in a stylishly messy French twist, and her outfit is classic college-girl-approaching-the-threshold-of-real-life. I want to ask where she found her vintage Coach bag, but now's not the time.

"Did you get the Pinterest page I sent with those flowers in mason jars?" I ask.

"Yes," she says slowly, glancing around like she expects a farm animal ambush. "They'd be pretty with rose gold ribbon."

"Absolutely." I flick a hand toward the imaginary tables. "Picture them with little stargazer lilies. Or maybe early-season tulips. Those should be available this time of year."

Julia's blue eyes continue a survey of the space, and I know she's seeing it in her mind.

The rustic wine barrels spilling with wildflowers.

The cute chalkboard signs pointing people to her guest book.

The train of her gown gliding through a pile of fresh reindeer droppings.

The beast responsible for the droppings snorts and rubs her branchlike antlers on a post.

"Tammy won't be invited to your ceremony," I assure the bride and groom. "We keep the reindeer penned up during weddings."

Tammy the reindeer stamps a hoof and keeps banging her antlers on the post. She's due to lose them any day now, and I say a silent prayer it won't happen in the next five minutes.

"It's totally fine, honey," the mother of the bride assures me. "The whole point of doing a rustic, country-style wedding is having some flavor."

"We can certainly offer that." I turn back to the happy couple. "We're all about the quaint, country charm."

The groom—who's been mostly quiet up to this point—takes his bride's hand and studies her face as intently as she's watching Tammy. "What do you think, honey?" he says. "It has that homey, folksy vibe going for it."

Julia does an agreeable little head tilt, though I can't tell from her face if she thinks that's a good thing or a bad thing. "I guess rustic country chic is all the rage right now." She glances at me for affirmation. "I see a lot of that on Pinterest."

I nod like a bobblehead, grateful for the powers of Pinterest in backing up my business plan. "Did you see last month's cover of *Bride* magazine? Country chic is in."

The mother of the bride puts a hand on her daughter's arm. "Remember that episode of *Say Yes to the Dress* where they had those adorable burlap table runners and centerpieces with bright red apples in little metal tubs?"

Tammy the reindeer swings her antlers our direction, and I hold my breath. She knows that word, and she's poised to stomp over here and start snuffing at pockets for Honeycrisps. I focus very hard on using mental telepathy to beg my sister to come drag the blasted reindeer out of the barn.

But since Jade and I aren't telepathic, Tammy just stares.

"It's nice, I guess," Julia says, with roughly the same enthusiasm I'd use to describe the work gloves I bought last week.

"I think it's totally charming." The groom squeezes her hand, and I can tell he really means it. "My family would say it's exotic."

"Exotic." Julia frowns a little. "That's because they're from Manhattan. It's not exotic when you spent childhood summers mucking stalls."

"Now, honey." The mother of the bride puts an arm around her daughter's shoulders and smiles at me. "It's a hat tip to your heritage."

"A way to blend our lives together." The groom smiles, then lowers his voice just a touch. "And we are sort of in a hurry."

The look they exchange confirms what I guessed the second these two first called about pulling off a wedding in five weeks.

My own furtive glance at his Allen Edmonds shoes and Ralph Lauren slacks fills out the rest of the picture: East Coast boy from old money knocks up college sweetheart whose middle-class upbringing comes from cattle ranching instead of blue chip stocks. Opposites attract, etcetera etcetera, and graduation's close enough that no one will question a hasty spring wedding.

"How about I email you some figures and a link to another Pinterest board with a few ideas I think you might like," I tell them. "That'll give you some time to talk things over."

The mother of the bride hoists her leather bag a touch higher on her shoulder. "That would be lovely, dear. Can I also get you to send us some more suggestions for catering? None of the ones you mentioned were quite what we're looking for."

"We're foodies," the bride says, smiling as she shoots an

adoring look at the groom. "Our first date was at Le Bernardin in New York City."

"Not a problem," I tell them, which isn't totally true. Catering options are limited in Central Oregon, especially this time of year. "I'll make some calls and see what I can find."

"Wonderful," chirps the mother of the bride. "We'll be in touch."

The three of them shuffle toward the door, and the groom holds it open for his betrothed. As the barn door closes, the bride's voice carries back to me in a hushed half-whisper.

"It's too bad that Ponderosa Luxury Resort place isn't open yet. That would be perfect."

Damn.

Well, we knew there'd be some overlap between the rustic country-style weddings we're offering and the plans for hoity rich person weddings at the ranch-turned-luxury-resort down the road. It's to be expected. We even met with their marketing VP to make sure no one's stepping on anyone else's toes, but still.

I turn and trudge out the door and into the paddock where my sister is busy shaving mud balls off the hindquarters of a large reindeer steer.

"This week on *Lifestyles of the Rich and Famous*," I announce. "The glamorous world of reindeer ranching."

Jade rolls her eyes and snips another mud ball. "You want to give me a hand here?"

I grin and step close enough to plant a kiss behind the reindeer's left antler. "Hey, Harold," I say as Jade maneuvers an especially large glob of muddy fur. "Are you glad you don't have to wear the Donner harness and jingle bells anymore?"

"So happy that he gave himself a mud bath," Jade mutters. "How'd it go with the wedding couple?"

"Tammy was very helpful."

"Crap, sorry. I thought I had her penned in."

"It's fine, she was mostly charming," I say. "Pretty sure the couple's going to sign on for that date in five weeks."

"Shotgun wedding?"

"That's my guess.

"God bless failed birth control," my sister says.

"It'll keep these guys in beet pellets and hay when they're not earning their keep on the Christmas circuit."

Jade snips another mud ball as Harold tosses his massive antlers in dismay. "I'm impressed we're already booking this many weddings."

"I *am* kind of impressive, aren't I?" My cheeky quip earns me a snort from my sister and a grunt from Harold. I give him a scratch behind one enormous antler. "I think the catering thing is going to be an issue."

"How so?"

"No one's doing the farm-to-table thing everyone wants. Not this time of year, anyway. Options are limited for gourmet snobs."

"It's winter in a high-desert mountain town," she points out. "The only thing growing right now is juniper."

"Juniper's good for gin."

"What else would anyone need for a wedding?" Jade snips another mud ball and looks thoughtful. "You know, Brandon's cousin is a Michelin-starred chef."

"The one doing the restaurant stuff at *Ponderosa Luxury Ranch Resort?*"

I give the words the proper socialite sneer, even though we've mostly stopped mocking the neighbors for plunking down a rich person's resort in the middle of freakin' farm country. The fact that my sister is boning a member of their family might have something to do with that.

"Sean's a great cook," Jade says. "Maybe he has time for a side job, since they're not opening for another couple months."

"Huh." I like this idea. "Plus winter's slow for everyone," I add. "And it could be a good way for them to get their name out there before they open." I rub my hands down the front of my jeans, eager to see if this could pan out. "I can give him a call and see what he says."

"Why don't you go in person," she says. "There's a turkey in the barn that I promised we'd deliver today."

"Alive or frozen?"

"Neither. It's that stuffed turkey grandpa shot when it attacked you in the driveway, remember?"

"The highlight of my toddlerhood." I kick at a dirt clod that looks like a misshapen penis, then feel bad when it crumbles to bits. "Why am I taking a taxidermied turkey to our new neighbors?"

"Some kind of photo shoot," Jade says. "Bree asked to borrow the turkey and one of Dad's old crossbows. They're thinking about offering turkey hunting trips for rich snobs who want to pretend they're outdoorsmen."

"Sounds like a good way for Percival to take an arrow through the hand."

"Percival?"

"That seems like a rich person's name, doesn't it?"

Jade looks thoughtful. "It's a good name for our next reindeer calf, actually."

I roll my eyes and turn toward the barn. "You're weird."

"Don't forget the turkey," she calls after me. "And the crossbow."

Words I never expected someone to yell at me when I graduated with honors from the U of O marketing department.

I trudge into the barn and locate the feathery beast, shuddering at the sight of it. I haven't seen the damn thing since third grade when I brought it to show-and-tell dressed in my mother's favorite bra and panty set. It was the first of several occasions my parents were asked to have a talk with me about the difference between appropriate and inappropriate public behavior.

I tuck the crossbow under my arm and spend a few moments figuring out the best way to carry the damn bird. The taxidermist posed it like it's poised to take flight, spreading its massive four-foot wingspan for full effect.

I settle for bear hugging it to my chest like the world's most awkward infant, and I heft it into the cab of the work truck for the five-minute drive to Ponderosa Luxury Ranch Resort.

For years, the place was the vanity ranch of an east coast billionaire who showed up a few times a year to play cowboy. It barely registered on my radar until the guy up and died, leaving the place to his adult kids, who've spent the last year quietly transforming it into a country-style luxury resort.

I have yet to see it in person. Running a reindeer ranch at Christmas doesn't leave much free time for tea and crumpets with the neighbors.

I pull through the massive wooden gates with the Ponderosa Luxury Ranch Resort logo spelled out in cast iron curlicue. The driveway is long and paved, which is the mark of extravagance this far out of town. Several massive, rustic-looking buildings line the drive, with signs announcing their intended purpose. There's the "Cedar Golf Club" and the "Aspen Springs Day Spa," and the "Tamarack Ballroom." I wonder if all those trees consented to having their names plastered on monuments to the wealthy.

I pull up in front of the biggest building of all, the one with a massive sign declaring it the Ponderosa Lodge and Luxury Suites. Beneath that is a smaller sign indicating it's also the home of Juniper Fine Dining. The whole building is designed to look like a vintage barn, but at ten times the size and with twenty times the windows. The water feature beside the front door probably cost more than my college education.

I park the truck and get out, then turn to grab my creepy welcome gifts. With the turkey hugged to my chest and the crossbow wedged awkwardly under one arm, I make my way along the paver-stone pathway to a set of massive glass doors that must be fifteen feet tall.

Hesitating a moment, I tap the bottom of the door with the toe of my boot. Not much of a knock, but the door swings open anyway. Automatic? Must be.

I step through it in a rush of light and sage-laced breeze, hoping I'm not walking right into someone's living room. The place isn't open to the public yet, so I'm not sure what to expect.

"Hello," I call out, squinting against the bright sunlight crashing down on me from all four sides. Good lord, it's going to cost a fortune to keep these windows clean. "Hellloooo?"

I blink hard, struggling to see anything through the flood of sunlight and the bundle of turkey feathers in my arms. There's a figure up ahead, a man. He's standing on a ladder, and as my eyes start to adjust, I realize "man" might be an understatement.

The dude is ripped. Broad shoulders, rounded biceps, and a build that could land him on the cover of *Men's Fitness*. The scruff on his face is the color of toasted cinnamon, and the hand that grips a screwdriver is the size of a dinner plate. His hair is sandy and tousled like someone's just run her fingers through it.

My fingers twitch at the thought of being that someone.

He turns and squints my direction, blinded by the force of the solar explosion gushing from the windows around me. As he blinks against the flood of light, I get a good look at his eyes. Good lord, the color. Not just green, but a deep, shimmery bottle-green like glass glinting in the sun.

My mouth goes dry, and I stand there like an idiot while the guy gapes at me in silence.

"Holy shit," he says.

And then he passes out.

. . .

***

Want to keep reading? Grab *Chef Sugarlips* here! https://books2read.com/b/3L0aqw

DON'T MISS OUT!

Want access to exclusive excerpts, behind-the-scenes stories about my books, cover reveals, and prize giveaways? You'll not only get all that by subscribing to my newsletter, I'll even throw you a **FREE** short story featuring a swoon-worthy marriage proposal for Sean and Amber from *Chef Sugarlips.*

Get it right here.

http://tawnafenske.com/subscribe/

ACKNOWLEDGMENTS

Endless hugs and thanks to my street team, Fenske's Frisky Posse, for being the world's most wonderful cheering section, sounding board, and assembly of unpaid marketing experts. I love you guys!

Big kudos to Kait Nolan for holding my hand, formatting my book, and coaching me through this whole process (and for writing kick-ass books to boot!) I couldn't have done this without you.

I'm also incredibly thankful for Linda Grimes, who never hesitates to critique me at a moment's notice, and who never fails to make my books better. Smooches and hugs to Meah Meow for doing double-duty as an awesome author assistant and the world's best pet sitter.

Thanks also to Susan Bischoff and Lauralynn Elliott of The Forge for all the fabulous editing work on Christmasbitch. Er, I guess we should start calling it by the real title?

I'm eternally grateful to Cindy Murdoch of Timberview Farm for patiently answering all my reindeer questions and for letting me into your fascinating world of hooves and antlers. You're amazing! Thanks also to Operation Santa Claus for all the childhood reindeer memories. Any mistakes or liberties I've taken in my descriptions of reindeer rearing are mine alone.

Love and thanks to my family, Aaron "Russ" Fenske and Carlie Fenske, and Dixie and David Fenske for a lifetime of support and fabulous holiday memories. Thanks also to Cedar and Violet for showing me how much more fun Christmas can be with the pitter-patter of non-pet feet.

And thanks especially to Craig, for not only doing the normal supportive husband-of-an-author thing, but also jumping in as cover artist, visual media expert, sounding board, masseur, counselor, and one-man graphic design team. I can't possibly thank you enough, but I have a few ideas for giving it a shot. Love you, babe!

ABOUT THE AUTHOR

When Tawna Fenske finished her English lit degree at 22, she celebrated by filling a giant trash bag full of romance novels and dragging it everywhere until she'd read them all. Now she's a RITA Award finalist, *USA Today* bestselling author who writes humorous fiction, risqué romance, and heartwarming love stories with a quirky twist. *Publishers Weekly* has praised Tawna's offbeat romances with multiple starred reviews and noted, "There's something wonderfully relaxing about being immersed in a story filled with over-the-top characters in undeniably relatable situations. Heartache and humor go hand in hand."

Tawna lives in Bend, Oregon, with her husband, step-kids, and a menagerie of ill-behaved pets. She loves hiking, snowshoeing, standup paddleboarding, and inventing excuses to sip wine on her back porch. She can peel a banana with her toes and loses an average of twenty pairs of eyeglasses per year. To find out more about Tawna and her books, visit www.tawnafenske.com.

ALSO BY TAWNA FENSKE

The Ponderosa Resort Romantic Comedy Series

Studmuffin Santa

Chef Sugarlips

Sergeant Sexypants

Hottie Lumberjack

Stiff Suit

Mancandy Crush (novella)

Captain Dreamboat

Snowbound Squeeze (novella)

Dr. Hot Stuff

The Juniper Ridge Romantic Comedy Series

Show Time

Let It Show

Show Down (coming soon!)

Just for Show (coming soon!)

Show and Tell (coming soon!)

Show of Hands (coming soon!)

The Where There's Smoke Series

The Two-Date Rule

Just a Little Bet

The Best Kept Secret

Standalone Romantic Comedies

At the Heart of It

This Time Around

Now That It's You

Let it Breathe

About That Fling

Frisky Business

Believe It or Not

Making Waves

The Front and Center Series

Marine for Hire

Fiancée for Hire

Best Man for Hire

Protector for Hire

The First Impressions Series

The Fix Up

The Hang Up

The Hook Up

The List Series

The List

The Test

The Last

Standalone novellas and other wacky stuff

Going Up (novella)

Eat, Play, Lust (novella)

CPSIA information can be obtained
at www.ICGtesting.com
Printed in the USA
LVHW081344280222
712219LV00020B/182

9 781979 770682